THE SOVEREIGNTIES OF INVENTION

T0154196

Thank you Josh Glenn

Library of Congress Control Number 2012930689

Book Design by Kate Gavriel
Cover by Goodloe Byron
Printed in the United States of America

Red Lemonade
a Cursor publishing community
Brooklyn, New York

www.redlemona.de

Versions of many of these stories first appeared at
Hermenaut.com and HiLoBrow.com
Distributed by Publishers Group West

ISBN 978-1-935869-12-2

10 9 8 7 6 5 4 3 2 1

THE SOVEREIGNTIES
OF INVENTION

tales by
Matthew Battles

Red Lemonade
a Cursor publishing community
Brooklyn, New York
2012

CONTENTS

The Dogs in the Trees   3

The Sovereignties of Invention   10

The Gnomon   18

The Manuscript of Belz   26

Time Capsules   37

Camera Lucida   47

For Provisional Description of Superficial Features   59

I After the Cloudy Doubly Beautifully   73

Passages   86

The Unicorn   95

The World & the Tree   102

THE DOGS IN THE TREES

The first sightings of dogs in trees were reported not long after the Fall equinox. Early rumor came in the form of videos shot at arms' length on cell phones and hastily uploaded—grainy, shaky, made with cock-angled intensity, the palsied depth of field swimming as it sought purchase amidst limbs and leaves. I regarded these links with bemused curiosity, reloading and watching again in a couple of instances to search for telltale lumber or wires or other evidence of trickery. But no more than a week had passed before I witnessed the sight firsthand. In a great pin oak by the corner of my street, in the crook of a heavy branch full thirty feet off the ground, a greyhound brown as bark stared at me with that expression of mingled curiosity and resignation which so many dogs are wont to wear.

I stood beneath the dog for some while; its coat of dark brindle blended into the background, and I had to blink to separate figure from ground. The tree itself was a beautiful specimen, which surely had stood in the district since long before the first houses had been built. It would have seen and survived the clearing that turned a tangled wood into an estate of copse and meadow, would have witnessed the subsequent laying out of streets, their pavement in wood and brick and macadam, and the rise of homes that rivaled but did not overmatch its ever-spreading height. Thanks to the clumsy landscaping of the bank along the road, the oak now rose out of the earth seemingly at mid-trunk, without the arched and mossy root-flare a tree of such stature usually exhibits. Rising out of the ground at its full circumference, the tree seemed as if it might reach down any number of yards through loam to bedrock or beyond to root in worlds beyond reckoning, dimensions in which clay and loam were transparent as the air into which the tree's top jutted. The canopy still held its full complement of barbed and elegant leaves. Tiny acorns lay all about on road and lawn alike, ground on the pavement to a soft brown flour by the passage of cars. A stately oak, as the formula goes, a neighborhood tree utterly unremarkable but for the prodigy of a dog, sleek and pacific, nestled amidst the buttresses of the canopy—a prodigy out of which the wonder of the tree itself seemed to erupt, seemed to speak.

A prodigy in any case for the lack of evident means by which the dog could have assumed its seat; for no steps, no rope-and-pulley setup, no basket or bungee were visible. Nor was the tree's tightly furrowed bark marred by any trace that claws would have left— as any canid climbing to such heights would needs have fought a terrific battle, would have done itself and the tree great violence. But the dog, although somewhat discomfited by the precariousness of its position, showed no other sign of disarrangement or dis-ease. As I stood far below it broke off staring at me, yawned, stretched, turned its head demurely and dropped into the kind of haunch-raised crouch that greyhounds seem to prefer. The great branch ever so slightly shivered to its leafy ends, signaling the shift in weight, the tree registering the unavoidable empirical quiddity of a dog in its midst.

After standing for some time beneath the dog in the tree, I summoned the consciousness to pass beneath and continue on my way to work. In the office where my colleagues and I ran a small free daily journal, the trickle of reported sightings already had captured our attention. Having been the first to witness the phenomenon (at any rate, the first to admit to it), I was assigned to cover a situation that was growing stranger and more engrossing by the hour.

Late the following afternoon, on the strength of numerous testimonies, I made my way to a nearby park. Most of the land there, which stretched between two boulevards flowing with traffic, was taken up by a pair of ballfields separated by a grove of trees that following a low narrow bourne through which a bit of slime might trickle on soggy winter days. This day was dry, however, and the trees, mostly Norway maples, stood tall as their bright leaves spiraled down to gather in drifts in the long grass. Hanging like ornaments amidst the boughs, a veritable pack of pooches in all shapes and sizes—nine dogs of various breeds and ages—regarded their growing audience of humans with innocent eyes. Wedged into lichen-spangled, deep-foundationed crooks were a sleek Labrador and what I took to be a malamute; further out, a spaniel set its branch swaying with the wagging of its tail; in the next tree a wiry-haired mongrel with a lazy eye looked down over its wedge-shaped snout; and two Pomeranians, white as down, seemed to float like clouds netted in the woody tangle. At the farthest extent of several limbs bobbed a cockeyed chihuahua, a trembling poodle, and a pekingese, its hair flowing over the end of the branch almost decoratively.

Cur and purebred alike festooned the copse like notes on a musical staff, and the people pondered them and murmured to one another sotto voce like concert-goers. It was a bright Fall day, and warm, and the crowd had grown; office workers were sitting in the grass with their food in their laps. Most were on their phones either talking or taking pictures. A vendor pulled up at the curb and offered tacos from an insulated box nestled in the trunk of his car. A few children ran here and there, evidently unconcerned for the dogs, as if they alone among the tribe of mankind were unmoved by the strange scene. The dogs watched all this with some interest; it was evident that several were hungry, as they licked their lips and quivered with attention while the taco vendor plied his goods.

It was afternoon, and school was letting out; among the arriving children some teens lurked, snickering and aloof. A loose knot of them now broke away to lope towards the dogs, gathering speed as they crossed the grassy hillside; nearing the trees, they launched a salvo of rocks. The dogs were quite high, some topping seventy-five feet from the ground; the rocks reached apogee and seemed to waver before plunging harmlessly back toward the boys, who dodged and laughed and punched one another. The dogs backed up against the trunks or—where no retreat was possible—looked left and right in beseeching submission. The crowd had quieted; there was a tension, as all pondered the question whether to intervene. It seemed to me that the question prompted others—for why merely stop the boys from throwing rocks? Why had no one called for a ladder, or dialed 911 and asked for the fire department? They come for cats, after all. Why had they not come for the dogs? What is to be done about the dogs in the trees? I pondered these questions as I stared hard at the dogs themselves, not scrupling to look left or right to those standing with me in the field, sensing the current of avoided eye contact rippling through the crowd.

On the boulevards cars flowed without cease, a sibilant, breathless hiss. The boys, oblivious of everything but the maddening, insistent absurdity of the dogs on high, threw stones with a stiffening intensity, silent now but for their grunts of effort. Together they crackled with a threat that had stopped thinking and was now intent upon its task. The only thing that could destroy this hate would have been the ugly success of their endeavor; and yet the dogs remained just out of rocks' reach, their defenses fully deployed. The pack instinct bloomed among them now; they growled and snapped cowered in vain attempts at succor or submission. One of the pekingese began to bark, not angrily but plaintively it seemed, swaying there upon its perch; the boys turned their aim its way with redoubled energy, the rocks now reaching the heights and looping over the pooch in sharp, threatening arcs. I nearly called out then, fighting the thickening in my throat, coughing and all but barking myself—when out of the wind fell a flock of starlings, rippling and distending, diving towards the copse. It flowed as a freshet around the boys, who stood frozen in the hurtle of birds swooping upwards, whirling and braiding their passage into the steel blue sky before settling in an instant upon every branch amidst the copse. At this wordless chastening the boys dispersed, and the crowd's brittle energy fractured into small shards of conversation, voices respectfully quiet as in a church or a hospital before the bird-beatified dogs.

By degrees, however, such scenes lost their distinctiveness. As the number of dogs in trees continued to grow, the sense of prodigy gave way to a siege of numbing tension. At first it had seemed that only the lost, the stray, and the feral were taking to the canopy; with regularity now people reported their own dogs had gone missing in the trees. A neighbor's blue-pointed cattle dog, whose face had always seemed to me to bespeak a placid certainty, had resisted the call for some weeks; but from day to day for some while now it had watched through the windows with unappeased fervor as the trees swayed in the seasonal winds and gave up their leaves. The pooch—Pearly was its name—had all but ceased eating or even drinking water, and would no longer walk on its leash, but would only stand with its lips trembling at the base of the first tree it encountered. My neighbor greeted these behaviors with undisguised consternation, her anguish taking the form of impatience with Pearly's new-found, metastasizing madness. She would stand at the foot of a great wart-kneed beech berating Pearly, who crouched in tremulous rapture, tugging and tugging at the leash until it seemed the poor dog would lose consciousness, until at last Pearly would back away down the path towards home. At night, my neighbor told me, Pearly no longer slept at the foot of the bed; instead she paced at the door, stopping only to paw and whine piteously. She would turn in unsettled circles, coming round each time with freshened purpose as she caught a glance of bough-shadow twitching in the moonlight, or sniffed who knows what subtle allusion of bark and leaf-litter. Her whimpering turned to barking, which by degrees lengthened into a mournful baying for which Pearly seemed to have no lack of energy. Three nights this full-throated cry went on; I could hear it on the cold air, joined now and again by dogs on high throughout the neighborhood. Looking through the window above my bed, I caught glimpses of baleful eyes staring in the sky, their livid green constellating the dark high fretwork of the trees.

On the third night Pearly's plaint went quiet. I found out a few days later that my neighbor, having reached the nadir of her patience, had in the end simply opened the door. Opened the door and watched as Pearly flowed into the night without another sound.

And on it went, the dogs abandoning their families and friends and taking to the trees. No one could explain how, much less why, they made their way up the trunks and into the branches; no one seemed ever to catch them in the act of climbing or vaulting or perhaps even flying skyward to light among the branches. And day by day the dog's domestic career gave way to this new arboreal habit. Trees drooped with—what, not packs—gangs? flocks? Limbs grew heavy with their canine crop: dogs haunting the branches in silence, swaying in the wind; dogs shivering but stoic in the cold gray mornings; dogs in trees, their shoulders swathed in growing cowls of snow.

By midwinter they were dying. Rarely did the bodies lie about for long; municipal authorities dispatched crews to patrol the tree-lined streets, gathering up the remains and carrying them off in covered trucks. Occasionally, they struck a car or broke a fence in their falling, but such deaths were infrequently witnessed. For the most part, people had lost their fascination; videos stopped making their way around the networks, and news coverage all but ceased. I was soon reassigned to writing movie reviews, a happy respite in those wet, dark months. By the time the first buds of Spring had burst open with their bright and larval leaves, the dogs were gone. And in the years since, we talk about them hardly at all. The dogs have left us, the consensus seems to be; their rebuke is quiet and complete, and may only be passed over in silence. Few now will admit to having ever owned a dog, fewer to having lost one. To the children, dogs are a rumor—an archetype, a figment fit for dreaming—like the other lost creatures who once filled the skies and darkened the plains.

THE SOVEREIGNTIES OF INVENTION

He stood there with the box torn open, torn ribbons of tape and flaccid little packing-bags strewn about on the table. And in the midst of this mess, the prize—the shiny tool itself, pregnant with possibility transcending mere size or evident simplicity. Just this: a smooth black box of lucite sheen trailing a cord from which depended two earpieces that were more like some minimally-invasive pieces of diagnostic equipment than an audiophile's earbuds. He held them up, watched as their pliant, flesh-colored cords unwound themselves. The ends of them were made out of some fashionably late-technology rubber, like silicone but for the porosity, of somewhat shocking length and hooked at the ends. There was in the examination a slight thrill as he imagined how they would feel in his ears with the biomorphic nubs hooking, twisting, urging themselves deeper into the auditory canal. They're for more than mere listening, these probes. He knew that much. That's why he ordered the device. The whole package is much more promising, curiosity-piquing, flat-out intriguing, than the latest audio fantasia. This is a tool that goes straight to the heart of the matter.

The need had proceeded the desire, which had only taken form while jogging through the park the week before while ideas ran, as ever, faster than memory could sieve them from the flow. How to catch them? If only there were some technology for catching the stream of consciousness itself. Like dictation software, only more immediate, less troubled with corporeal vagaries. Try running and speaking into a microphone; between the jarring strides and the ever-quickening roar of the breath, any jogger's monologue would be software-unintelligible. No, a sip from the stream before it's embodied, that's the thing—a bugging of the mind, an eavesdropping on the song of the homunculus himself up there in his cranial habitat cool and removed.

A quick search, a gnomically-worded advertisement led to the right of results. Of course—there *is* a tool for this! Brain-hacking, thy time has come! It was a prospect that only had awaited the necessary reduction in circuit size, the requisite blooming of processing speed. Once upon a time in some mad laboratory there must have been machine-age versions—big as locomotives, only stationary—wired to craniums through god-knows-what steampunk fiendishness of clamps and buckles and screws. But this is the twenty-first century! No need for piercing, unless for purposes of adornment. The trick is simple now—a matter of pure wave, sympathetic resonance, good vibrations. Like barcodes or free broadband wireless, the stream of consciousness was a natural resource, clean and endlessly renewable, which merely awaited the advent of the right tool to pry mind from brain and deliver it to its user.

Instructions were printed in a confusion of languages and scripts on an intricately-folded sheet of onionskin; he tossed it on the table. He knew from the buzz on the tech blogs how the thing worked (or at any rate how it was to be worked; its inner workings, its clusterfuck of byzantine intellectual property and nondisclosure agreements and blackboxed kluges—like the evolved plumbing of the brain itself—were all but irrelevant). At either end were centered two ports for the headset cords: one for input, the other for output. Plugged into the input end, the earprobes would record one's stream of consciousness, download it onto a precious token of highly purified solid-state memory. Plug into the output end, and one's own thoughts would come streaming back in the fullness of their inspirational originary glory. The whole of the glossy black case was touch-sensitive; by means of subtle pettings and fingerings, a kind of tuning of the recorded mindstream would be effectuated. No need for instructions, in short; instead of wasting time reading them, he would suit up and head out on a run. Spandex snugged down, sweat-stinking jersey of ceramic-core titanium threaded fabric zipped and velcroed into place, gel-sprung shoes cinched tightly with surgeons' knots and then—earprobes inserted slowly, twistily, going in cold but quickly warming—out the door.

Running toward the park, he found his thoughts were occupied with the sensations induced by the probes. There was a slight tingling, almost a sleeplike numbing sensation, not altogether unpleasant, where sensation should not arise. And with it, a subtle tugging, or pressure—no, more like a sucking, somewhat akin to a kiss. Noting these phenomena as he rounded the corner and the park swung into view, he realized that he was musing on the device rather than thinking thoughts worthy of its extraordinariness. Would this be the dilemma of the new age to come? Constantly testing one's ever-more-intimate mental and imaginal exertions against the beauty of the tools we use to extract them? Let it be so, he thought—make it a goad, and not an accusation.

And by degrees his conscious thoughts ran on to more immediate things. Small protestations of ache from the right knee when rounding corners. Windrows of leaves gathered along the park fence, soggy and dank in the shadows of the trees but golden and wind-fluffed in the sun; the smell of diesel exhaust from a far-off mulching machine doing its work over yonder hill; parenthetical shadows of crows on the brightening ground. Dales and rocky embrasures winked among bare trees suggesting little independent kingdoms, micro-states in potentia, haunts and aeries for the mind's fancies. And here—a flit of inspiration, a connective arc of the mind in motion—a metaphor for the work of artists, the topic of a piece of writing for he was searching for, something sufficiently free of banality to serve as a framework or launching stage. And here it was—but what was it? Something about artists seeking out their independent sovereignties of invention. A turn of phrase to conjure with! he thought as he crested a hill and headed into the trees. He hoped he could remember the words until he reached home—but at the thought he felt the kissing sensation freshen in his ears and broke into an open-mouthed, hyperventilated smile. Reassured, he kicked down the backside of the hill and followed his accustomed route round the park and homeward, browsing the standard catalogue of sights and sensations. Thoughts and images arose and receded: dark women pushing light-hued babies in strollers; trickle of sweat cold down the spine; a flicker of headstones through the wrought-iron fence across the road from the park. And so on through the paces of another unhurried run.

Once home, however, excitement gripped him again. He quickly showered and toweled off, then ran back downstairs to the living room, where the recorder lay sleek as a seal on the coffee table. Slipping the earprobes back into place, he pulled the cord from the input jack, flipped the device around, and slid the jack into the output hole.

Instantly he was in a jacking, hinged world of pain—not so much a world as a room, sleeved in darkness, socketed to a pulsating elsewhere of dim relevance—he was converted to a snapping zither of connective tissues, wracked with dissonant chords of friction and rupture—blighted zones of craze and hollow, torrents of apocalyptic inflammation. Where were hips, arms, head? Lost in the nothing now beyond this polarity of pain, snapping like a toothless jaw caught in the trap of itself, hungering and hurting—

He found he was lying on the floor, fœtally curled, drenched in fresh cold sweat. The earprobes were still fixed in place, but the recorder lay on the rug just out of grasp. It must have slipped out of his hand when he fell—but how had he fallen, and why? He cast his mind back to a moment before, and felt sick to his stomach. What had gone wrong? Was the device broken? What kind of thought would produce such agony? Slowly he pushed up to a sitting position—and as he did so, a faint ache pinged through his right knee. It was like the faintest recollection—an echo minute but precise— of the astonishing, disembodied pain that had possessed him when he plugged the earprobes into the output.

Still shaky, he rose and went to the table, where the device's instruction sheet still stood on the points of its pleats in a doglike, hopeful stance. Scanning the words crammed into tiny, tightly-spaced paragraphs in various languages, he found the English and scanned it. "The device picks up signals from the entire cranial network, with many sympathetic fields emanating from throughout the nervous system," it read. "Thus making it necessary to tune into the desired stream of consciousness. Unconscious thoughts and sensations will interfere with a pure signal." The instructions went on to describe how subtle movements of the thumb and fingers across the glossy covering of the device would set up electrical fields by which the user could search the synaptic streaming signals. "Without manual contact," the instructions continued," the circuit is not closed and no signal will be detectable." He returned to the living room where the device lay on the floor, cord loosely coiled and detached from the device altogether. Sitting cross-legged, he parked the device against the wall, put the earprobes back in place, and slowly inserted the jack into the port again, this time without making contact with the device itself. Then—reassured by the calm that still reigned in his world—he reached out and delicately touched one fingertip to the black glossine.

A trickle of moisture, conducted along the surface tension of a saline layer of water mere molecules deep, made its way from follicle to follicle down the hollow of his back. As it flowed downward it left a trail of water behind, of which he could detect the minutest variations in salinity and specific gravity as the individual water molecules gained the energy for evaporative liftoff. Thrills of pure sensation traveled down the hair shafts, which he could count precisely and instantaneously. A waxy cuticle of oil and epidermal debris seemed to congeal in the flow of sweat, which fanned out into a kind of delta of rills and rivulets among the finer hairs in the small of his back. He pondered those hairs individually and in association; he considered the somewhat-drier hairs beyond the great saline delta, and counted as well the fibers in his shirt where they rubbed and broke the flow of this river of sweat, which rippled and eddied in an endless contemplation of fluid music—

He lifted his finger. The room was dark, his entwined legs frozen, tingling. He felt hungry. How many hours had passed? And yet it had hardly been enough; he had barely begun to trace out the many rivulets, the droplets like lakes erect and individual, the flora that thrived in the waxiness that slathered the epidermis . . . a lifetime's study offered itself in what he remembered as a single fleeting sensation, one that barely triggered a conscious thought. And yet he knew now that it had taken place 1.31 miles into his run.

The possibilities suggested by this revelation made his head swim with nausea and hunger. Almost as if searching solid purchase, he dropped his finger back onto the device and pivoted its sensitive pad ever so slightly on its surface. The shadow of a crow danced among blades of grass, plucking them like harp strings, shuttering and releasing rays of light diffracting through chlorophyll and casting spectral rays dissolving into green. A quivering twist of the fingertip brought the percussive life of the ball of his foot swimming to the surface: pressure, release; pressure, release. The slightest upward slide brought the epiglottis into focus as the wind roared past and unnamed muscles strove to marshal and shape the flow of mucus and saliva. At the seizure of a cough—but even the cough opened a door to a world of sensation; he peered in and saw the whole perceptual libraries of triggers and reaction-states and responses—the cough caused him to break contact with the device and quickly regain it in the left auditory nerve, which intently delivered news of a symphony of white noise modulating as the head bobbed washing air in and out of the ear canal, or swiveled left and right changing the whole timbre of the universe—

In the small hours he staggered to the kitchen with the cords dangling around his neck and managed to eat a stick of butter. This was among the last composed and swaddled sensations he ever had. Days later he was found and taken to the hospital emaciated, his face a rictus of contemplation. His family moved him to an institution with stately grounds and simple rooms. He was allowed to keep the device, to which he was devoted; the staff, like the family who soon ceased to visit, could only wonder what strange music it yielded to him. He spent his life in twitching obeisance to the device, which ever afterwards he piloted through the immense interbricolated labyrinths of sensation harvested from that single late-fall jog. There were whole sociologies and psychologies of child-rearing to disentangle among the strollers; untold lives and losses to disinter amidst the graven names and dates of half-glimpsed headstones (and beyond the memories of the departed, the life cycles of lichens on the stones themselves, and the rock's own stories of sedimentation and upheaval in the deeps of time). But the stream of consciousness itself—the train of thought, that coil of inspired fire—this remained elusive. Whether it lay buried in some vault of percepts, or whether it trickled out in a flickering delta and evaporated, he never discovered. And gradually his mind grew entirely disarticulate; unconcerned with consciousness, identity, and even mere homeostasis; ever more estranged from the sovereignties of invention.

THE GNOMON

Inside the conference hall, it was all buzz and business. Vaporous lights girdled the high rafters; queues formed and broke, stirring with restless energy; sandwich wraps and skewered fruit arrived on platters. T-shirt tycoons and skittle-eyed wannabes trolled the floors, their IDs windmilling from multicolored lanyards. Sunlight filtered in from on high, beyond the banks of escalators giving on broad atriums that pattered with the sound of soft shoes and falling water. And for awhile at least, it seemed as if the hungers of the mundane world could be held at bay—as if possibility still reigned—as if the vexing present, too, were unevenly distributed, and the horrors, biding their time, receded beyond the horizon of the week.

I had joined the swishing queues and collected my badge; now I wandered aimlessly, fiddling with my lanyard, trying to puzzle out the meaning behind its pleasant purple color, wondering what inscrutable caste it signified. My presentation (on crowdsourcing distributed libraries of emotional solidarity) was scheduled for the next day, which left me with a night to kill. I could wander the city's tourist district, check out the trade show exhibits, or return to my room to see what was on cable. I was on my way to the escalators when a friend, Dirado Z_., caught my eye through a crowd of nerdcore groupies and waved me over. When I told him I wanted to head back to the hotel for a nap, he feigned astonishment, reporting that he planned to have a look at something called "The Gnomon" before the show floor got too busy. When I only cocked my eyebrow in reply, he grabbed my shoulder and steered me towards the exhibits.

The exhibition booths were contrived of the standard vanity fair—spike-haired suits stood in carpeted booths extolling the virtues of server racks and search engines, HD webcams and ergonomic furniture. One booth featured a kind of foam-block recliner wired up to record an impression of your body, to be transmitted as a sketch-up to a factory in China, where a bespoke office chair would be extruded from massive 3D printing machines. I watched Dirado recline in the spongy block for a full minute while his bodyform was recorded, soft techno sifting from expensively small speakers overhead.

After a meandering search, we found our way to "The Gnomon," which sat on a sleek pedestal in a small untenanted exhibition booth near the center of the hall. A black cube—though "black" is a term entirely inadequate to name the uncanny depths it expressed—it appeared to be fashioned of some kind of mineral, more likely living stone than any manufactured composite. The thing measured perhaps a cubic foot, and appeared for all the world perfectly solid—although its solidity seemed to signal a daunting weight balancing there upon the narrow column of the pedestal. Its Euclidean solidity was dizzying, almost horrifying; into its perfect planes one felt or dreamed oneself beginning to fall. I leaned in close, my toes cantilevering beneath me to hold my balance: the surface appeared not precisely uniform, but scaled, dappled with interlocking aureoles of obscurely crystalline difference. The scaling seemed to drop away inward, and my eye wanted to slide down through the subtle striations forever. Transcending the fuzzy aureolar array were larger patterns—fluid deltas, glacial black tides compounded of depths and time beyond reckoning. It was as though a prism from the core of a future earth—a planet whose ancient fires were banked, whose torsions of magma had stilled and gone dark—had been sectioned away and deposited here upon a pedestal flanked by two potted palms, which rustled and toiled in the center's turbulent forced air.

We wondered if it was some new kind of server configuration, perhaps a cloud storage medium or wireless technology. But the thing seemed to have no socket or dock, no antennae or proximity hubs, no interface, no display. It didn't even seem to draw on any external power source. The booth was similarly inscrutable, offering no indication of purpose, no documentation at all besides the riffling ripstop banner with the word GNOMON printed in tasteful type hanging overhead. But something about the abyssal, faintly sparkling quoz of the thing kept Dirado and me transfixed there for—for how long? Time slipped. Others arrived. When I tore myself away, a sizable crowd had formed; I stalked back to the escalators with the heat of many bodies soaked into my clothes. Only when I had reached the upper-level atrium did it strike me as strange that no one had dared reach out to touch The Gnomon.

The rest of the evening passed as I had expected: dinner and drinks with people I knew only from the web, followed by a desultory rave. At dinner, a woman checking her phone murmured that The Gnomon had friended her. And by the time we reached the party, it seemed everyone was checking to see whether The Gnomon was friend or follower; whether the stream of speculative #gnomon tweets contained any plausible information; and who was currently sharing location with the enigmatic black cube. It was the kind of buzz I recognized from other conferences, and it gave me a headache; alone, I made my way back to my room.

That night I lay beneath a heavy hotel duvet and listened to the hum of the air conditioner—a low oscillation, which contemplation revealed to be a work of parts. The dominant voice was baritone, throaty and sharp-featured, which rode a basso continuo that throbbed in the jaw. In their midst, weaving in and out of the waveforms, blew an airy, rattling descant of white noise blended with the faintest whiff of pitch. As I continued to lie stiffly beneath the covers, sweating and listening, a long polyrhythmic theme began to suggest itself. There was a pattern to this braided oscillation as low tones caught up with high and passed them, only to close in on one another again. As the patterns merged and the long periodicity drew to a close, a figure seemed to coalesce out of the glowering darkness—an image of blackness beyond the night, of plane converging on plane over uncanny depths. The Gnomon! As if the air conditioner music had summoned it, there it hovered—faint and transient but distinct in my mind's eye. And now I rolled and twisted; I fluffed the pillow and stuffed it between my knees; I flicked on the nightstand light and stared at the plaster overhead. But wherever my eyes came to rest, The Gnomon burned like an afterimage in black light.

I flung off the covers and paced the floor. As if riffing on the change in pressure, the air conditioner opened a fresh movement, a belching, didgeridoo drone. I stepped to the door and peered out into the hall; several people paced in their private nocturnal turmoils. I quietly pulled the door to and stood with my ear pressed against its cool enameled surface, wondering if they too were seeing The Gnomon. When sleep finally came, it was fitful and humid.

In the morning I made a tiny pot of coffee, pressed my shirt with the hotel iron, and strode from the room feigning refreshment. I was fine until I reached the conference hall; having arrived early for my talk, I stopped in the atrium to look out upon the show floor. A concentrated, corpuscular bustle seemed to be gathering amidst the exhibits, centered (surely, I thought) on The Gnomon. I watched, letting my eyes swim out of focus, until the phone in my pocket chimed its alarm, letting me know that it was time for my talk to begin. I shook off the stupor and headed for the upper floors where the conference rooms were found.

The talk started out in promising fashion. My co-panelists were compelling and popular figures in the world of crowdsourced emotional solidarity, and from the sound of key-tapping in the room I could tell our audience was engaged in the presentation. But as our talk wore on, I found myself fighting to remember the topic. The room was warming, and seemed to hum; the key-tapping died off to a trickle. Noting a sudden darkness filling in my peripheral vision, I looked behind me: the screen, which had a moment ago been filled with bright, text-laden slides, had gone black—not the slack gray of an unlit screen but a projected black. A scaly, aureolar black of numberless depths.

At that moment a great tone rang throughout the building, clear and loud and deep and exceedingly musical, but of so peculiar a note and emphasis that everyone paused while its last overtones played out. And first by ones and twos, and then in a general throng, the audience wandered towards the door and streamed into the halls. Again and again the tone rang out, exciting the very finest hairs into sympathetic vibration. We presenters found ourselves drawn as irresistibly as our audience.

In the hall I found Dirado Z_. He was standing in a corner where the hall turned towards the show floor, cringing in an eddy of the human tide that filled the corridor. It's throbbing, he said, gripping my shirt with a wild look in his eye. It's calling to us! The tones seemed no longer to ring or tintinnabulate, but to blare; there was a harsh note mixed in that grew with each distinct pulse of sound. Dirado looked towards the exhibit hall, and his eyes goggled in horror; he clapped his hands to his ears and staggered off, slowly battling the current of conference goers now streaming towards the exhibit hall. I watched his half-bald head lurching in the patterned gloom, seeming to gather speed as Dirado made his way towards the atrium and then out-of-doors.

Following Dirado's example, I plugged my ears with my fingers, digging in until they were sore. The tones still reached me through my bones, but their power was diminished. And yet unlike Dirado, I fell in with the crowd, compelled by curiosity mingled with some residual compulsion. Shuffling with the horde, I turned a corner that gave on the landing from which the escalators dropped into the exhibit hall. There I stopped, transfixed by the scene that played out below me.

The people streaming down the escalators joined queues that bent themselves into arcs, forming a great churning spiral of humanity spinning slowly on its axis at the center of the hall. The exhibits themselves had been trampled; coils of crepe and drifts of royal blue fabric caught on the wreckage of shelving and folding chair, of splayed plastic and shattered veneer. The spiraling crowd shambled on through the ruins, dragging it with their feet, mixing it into so much particolored flotsam. And in their midst The Gnomon glowered: still erect upon its pedestal, a throbbing core of darkness dragging all towards it. In the spiral's innermost circle, hands reached out to touch the Gnomon, a wickerwork of arms turning slowly like the spokes of some inexorable wheel. Outward from the Gnomon jetted pullulating ribbons of black as if driven by some nameless wind; they whipped over the heads of the pilgrims, who raised their arms in supplication. The urge to follow was unbearable; I shut my eyes against it, knelt down and touched my forehead to the cool glass beside the escalator. And amid the terrible tolling and the rank odor of compulsion, the lights of the hall began to shut down, one by one; and the fascinating darkness grew until it held illimitable dominion over all.

THE MANUSCRIPT OF BELZ

The library is collapsing on itself, trying to digest itself. Renovation has turned the whole place into a vast construction site, where tradesmen build temporary walls surrounding temporary walls surrounding temporary walls, ad-hoc postindustrial labyrinths lit by bare bulbs encroaching on the bookstacks. Construction workers come into my office daily, sledgehammering pillars and propping them up again, removing thermostats, ceiling lights, and flooring. It's out of this maze of dust and incandescent light that Brko emerges, bearing apologies and a manuscript—the apologies for his intrusion, and the manuscript for his enrichment. Then again, I suppose that's what his apologies are really for, too.

Brko is a construction engineer; he wears a hard hat with a troubled Balkan state's flag taped to it. Day after day in the bowels of the library he demolishes walls with a front-end loader. I've seen him stumping down the halls, sweaty and swollen-faced, but haven't spoken to him until today. When he enters, I think he's here to knock the thermostat off the wall again. But he says nothing, only gazing at the stacks of old, leatherbound volumes heaped up on my desk. After awhile, he says, "my book is more beautiful than this. I can show you?"

I smile and nod, thinking how little ever comes of such offers. But yes, I tell him, I'd love to see it, of course.

"It is here," he says, handing me a dingy manila envelope.

"But I thought it was a book," I say.

"Well, yes, it is piece of book. A page. But it is very beautiful. You look, maybe library will to buy."

The single leaf slides out easily; singed fragments of paper rain down upon the floor. But yes, it is beautiful—a nearly whole first page of a richly illuminated manuscript. I sit awhile stunned, burned by the iridescence of the gold leaf, the lapis whorls of the *abjad*. I want to know where Brko got it.

"Before I came, I was driver," Brko says. "I drove for UN, for journalists, for others, too—mostly at the end for UN inspectors. Someone gave to me. I knew it was beautiful. So I kept."

I wonder what else he knows about it.

"It comes from town called Belz," he tells me; "it had mosque, it had beautiful manuscript. Interior troops hit town hard, they break mosque down and burn. This the only page who survived."

I gaze a bit longer before handing the piece back to him. "It's beautiful," I say. "But we surely won't acquire it. We don't know its provenance—we can't know its origin with any certainty—and besides, it's incomplete, and badly damaged."

At this, Brko's face turns red. "Is this library telling me this, or you only? I am happy going someplace else."

I nod apologetically. "No no," I say. "I'm no expert. I would show your manuscript to someone who is."

And Brko slips the envelope on my desk and backs away, his head swaying to and fro. "Then we will see," he says. And with that, he exits.

I place a call to the curator of manuscripts. She's not answering, so I leave a voice mail and try to put the envelope out of my mind, to no avail. Late in the afternoon, I withdraw the delicate leaf from its sleeve and place it in a yellow puddle of lamplight. It is Ottoman, no doubt, masterfully done and prodigiously well-preserved; the parchment fresh, the ink all but moist. But where would it have come from, what sort of a place?

A little village in the rain. It always rained on Belz. This would have been the lore of the region, the prejudice against Belz, and the residents of the town would have shared it, even taken a perverse pride in it, perhaps. Why do I imagine such a downpour? Maybe I'm trying to forestall the fires, the bombing and burning that await the town and its manuscripts. In any case, *with the rain as with so much else, things had been this way as long as anyone in the country could remember. Even through the most difficult times of the Federated Republic and all that had followed, right up until the Nationalists took power, Belz would have been the same: a small town of white flaking walls, red tile roofs, and running gutters, framed by the chalky bulk of the mountain looming white amidst the clouds. Nearer to town would have stood the walnut orchards with their silken worm-bags hanging in the branches, the air pungent from the pulp of the fallen walnut husks mellowing in the Belz rain.*

In the center of town stood a mosque built of chips of stone taken from the mountain. It was very old, and had been beautiful once, the white rocks laced together with black mortar. During the Federated Republic, the stones of this same mountain, which in places bore the rough graffiti of Roman occupiers, were used all around the country to cover hillsides with great white letters that read out slogans like PARTY AND PEOPLE and the Grave Leader's name. These stones were Belz's second claim to fame—though the residents of Belz resented their renown in this matter, having been the conscripts who had carried those chips down the slopes in heavy baskets.

In the Federated Republic, the mosque had fallen out of use and into disrepair, and now it was a museum of sorts. Among a few old coins and shards of classical earthenware, it contained Belz's third most famous property, after the rain and the stones: the Manuscript of Belz. The people of Belz with their wet shoulders and their runny noses took great pride in this venerable book of scripture filled with calligraphy and ornamented with gold leaf and brilliant illuminations. Scholars came to Belz from as far away as the capital city to view and study the book. The town kept a small cell adjoining the display room in good repair, that scholars might have space in which to work and to spend a few nights if they so wished.

An old man, who fancied himself the keeper of the book, visited the mosque regularly to tidy the room and to attend to the scholars' needs. Though he could not make out the writing it contained—the old calligraphic styles never were prized for their legibility—he nonetheless loved to fondle it as it lay in its velvet cradle under glass. He made a ceremony of turning over a leaf of the manuscript each morning; this he did first thing, before going to the cell to dust its floor beams with a stiff broom. Sometimes he ran his rain-cracked fingertips over the loops and serifs of the characters, feeling the ridges the ancient pen had made as it had cut into the paper. He stared down at the illuminations, taking off his skullcap of roughly knitted wool and twisting it in his fists as he gazed wonderingly into the book.

When the Nationalists took power, the residents of Belz had cause to worry. Although they were not at all political—the Federated Republic and its Grave Leader had taken care of that—the Nationalists hated the Muslims, hated their skullcaps and their dark eyes, hated their distaste

for pork and strong liquor, hated the harsh fricatives of their dialect, all
so reminiscent of the heretical empire of old.

The curator of manuscripts arrives, interrupting my reverie.

"Let's have a look at this forgery your friend has brought you,"
she says as I hand her the envelope.

"A forgery," I ask? It's too bad. Of course, I'm not surprised to
hear it.

She slips the page from its cover, and the scent of burnt hide fills
the room. "I'm being unfair," she says. "It's not precisely a forgery—
more of a facsimile, really. And as the story goes, it was produced
for the best, most quixotic reason. You see, the people of the town
knew that the army was destroying all the Islamic objects they
could find, and they wanted to save their manuscript. So they hired
a conservator who knew the manuscript well, and he produced a
facsimile for them. The idea was to replace the original, to leave the
fake for the soldiers to find."

So if this is the fake, I wonder, what happened to the original?

The curator shrugs. "No one knows," she says. "According to
the prevailing opinion, the conservator must have absconded with
it. But Belz was razed only a couple of years ago. The volume could
still turn up, intact, in an auction somewhere." The curator holds
the piece at eye level, letting the lamplight plane off the prismatic
text. "It's shockingly good," she says. "I'll take it back to the lab for
a closer look, just to be sure. But you'll probably have to tell him he's
got a fine conversation piece."

The people of Belz knew that the Nationalists had begun their cleans-
ing; they saw tall stalks of black smoke rise and blossom on the horizon.
And the old man knew—for visiting scholars had told him—that the
Nationalists would burn the manuscript if it fell into their hands.

He brought the problem before the town council, who, naturally, were divided over the matter.

"They won't bother us here," one said. "When have they ever?"

"What about the young men?" one asked. "Each day another one goes to join the fighters in the hills. The troops will come when they find out about this."

"Couldn't we send the manuscript along with one of these boys?" someone asked in reply. "My nephew leaves tomorrow, nothing I've said will stop him."

"But what if he's caught?"

"My son is planning to pack his family and leave the country," said another. "He could take it with him."

"But they'll be stopped and searched at the border!"

"No no, the Interior Police won't bother with a simple family mulecart!"

"How can you hope to beat these thugs at their own games?" cried an older man. "When the troops arrive, we should welcome them with gifts of bread and salt in their custom. We should bow to them and hand over the manuscript. That way they won't burn our houses!"

"But no one can burn the houses of Belz!" someone said. He stood and shook his fist. "Our rain will stop them!" he shouted, and the crowd replied with hoots and peals of laughter.

The old man, who had stood patiently in the middle of the chamber through it all, shook his head, put his finger to his nose, and spoke. "I have a plan. Years ago a young scholar visited us. Now, this scholar, whose name was Fadim, I remember that he was also an artist. He told me that he knew how to write in the ancient calligraphic style of the manuscript, that he could bind the leaves into a book and sew a grand leather cover. Though this man had once worked in the capital city, he left when the university closed. He lives now with family not far from Belz. Now this Fadim, perhaps we can entice him to come, to make a facsimile of the manuscript that we can turn over to the police in place of the original."

The council argued awhile longer, but finally agreed to do as the old man suggested. The next day he borrowed a battered sedan from one of the councilors and drove over the pitted road to find Fadim and ask him to Belz.

Fadim was unhappy on his cousin's farm: afraid of the animals, repelled by the smells of the barn, he insisted that plowing and sowing should not be allowed to wreck his scholar's hands. Only when his cousin menaced him with a stick of wood for being such a useless wreck did he at last join in the work of the farm. He took refuge in solitary tasks, and even came to enjoy milking the cow—her udder leather-dry, her milk the same creamy yellow color as paper. Such opportunities for reverie were far-flung, however, and he passed through his days on the farm as if they were so many abandoned rooms. He squinted at the dirty children, cursing the country silence and the frozen stupidity of his cousin's people.

When the old man arrived from Belz, Fadim was perplexed. The venerable fellow made a strange ambassador, after all, with his moist skullcap and his sniffles. But at his first mention of Belz, Fadim's heart fluttered. His breath caught at the thought of the famous manuscript. And when the old man explained his mission, his invitation buoyed Fadim at once. He did not need to take a second glance at the bruised farm lying all around him before saying yes to the old man. He was careful, however, to mask his eagerness to leave, and his hunger to have the manuscript in his hands once again.

"We cannot pay you," the old man said. "But you will have use of the mosque, and free board for as long as you need."

Fadim pinched his chin and shook his head. "How much time do we have?" he asked. The old man only shrugged, for who could know? Perhaps the troops would never come—or perhaps they were in Belz already.

Fadim grumbled about his family and his duties on the farm, just to make a show of it. But in the end, of course, he told the old man he would come. It didn't even matter that Belz couldn't pay him, as the country's money was worthless. Belz offered honor, though, greater honor than he could ever find prodding his cousin's muddy sheep to return to their fold. So Fadim told his cousin he was leaving (the man only wiped his brow and spit on the ground) and packed a worn valise full of tools and materials and a bottle of cream fresh from the morning's milking. He placed his valise in the back seat of the sedan and settled in beside the old man, who sat behind the wheel eating a raw, peeled onion. The old man steered the car over the road, chattering on in his onion-scented fricatives about all the scholars who had ever visited Belz.

Belz welcomed Fadim like a martyr. The rain had dwindled to a premonitory mist; boys jumped up and down along the road playing their boom boxes as the car bumped up the steep hill toward the mosque. Some men roasted a goat while women linked their arms and danced in the muddy yard. The old man accompanied Fadim everywhere, smiling broadly and patting him on the back. Finally, he led him into the moist innards of the mosque, led him to the neat cell with its high desk and its window looking out on the gray skies and the houses of Belz fringed with the yellow-leafed crowns of the walnut trees. As the rain hammered the chipped stone wall outside, Fadim unpacked his needles and silken threads, his inks, and his pots of pigment and powdered gold.

Fadim began the labor thinking that his work need only be reasonably accurate. The Interior Police were infamous illiterates, criminals *released from the state prisons, and easily fooled. Any antique-looking book full of flourishes would satisfy their flames. But as he studied the manuscript—removed from its glass case and placed in its velvet cradle atop the high desk—Fadim was charmed once again by its sublime script. He read the holy words as if for the first time, and the manuscript spoke to him. He inhaled the incense of its antiquity—the dry, spiced scent of moldering paper and leather—until, when he fell into bed at night, he could smell it on his hands and in his hair. The figures of the script sang, made sounds of words the likes of which he had forgotten. How could he have missed all this beauty on his first visit to Belz? He was young then, of course, his graduate studies barely finished. And now, after all that had happened to him, he could see fresh milk and smell wet fields among the pages of the ancient text. In thrall to all this voluptuousness, he longed to reproduce it. He wanted nothing less than to recreate the Belz Manuscript—he would have stayed in that cell and made a thousand of them; he would have drawn and gilded and folded and sewn until he fell dead from the stool, had such a thing been possible. He would have filled the world with Manuscripts of Belz until they were plentiful as plums. And when the work was finished and the new manuscript lay atop the table beside its older twin, it seemed all the more glorious for its freshness. It lacked the scent of the old book, of course, but even that would come in time.*

The ringing phone interrupts my reverie. It's the curator of manuscripts.

"I have, well, interesting news, and then I have bad news," she says. "Bad news first: as I said, and as you thought, we can't really use the piece. It's fine, really, a first-rate example of the illuminations from its period. We can't firmly substantiate where it's from, as the manuscript was never microfilmed. So we don't know enough about it to curate it. But now, here's the interesting part: it's the real thing. It's not a facsimile. It's a genuine fifteenth century Ottoman manuscript, a fragment of the Koran, in fact."

"You're kidding. That's incredible."

The curator snickers into the phone. "You can tell your friend Brko to get in touch with me," she says. "I'll set him up with the someone at Sotheby's."

I remember that the Koran is an attribute of Allah, as perfect and eternal as His beauty, His anger, and His mercy.

I hang up the phone and stare at the heaps of books around me. Walls of precious, rare codices, safely immured in my library. Somewhere nearby, Brko knocks down a wall of bricks, and dust sifts from still more tomes as they tremble imperceptibly on their shelves. I suppose I should be surprised that Brko holds a piece of the original manuscript—that for all his attempts to pass a fake as the real thing, it proved to be authentic after all. Then again, perhaps the whole story of the facsimiles was a hoax, a confidence man's clumsy parable concocted to pique buyer Brko's interest.

I can't let go of Belz, though, or Fadim. I feel sure that Fadim was real, and that he had to betray Belz in the end. For would you not have felt, as Fadim must surely have felt, that such a work—a work of one's own hands, after all, the consummation of a lifetime's perfection of the rarest and most esoteric skills—could never be given over to the flames? Surely this is what Fadim felt. And surely this is why, *on that last wet morning before the sun had risen, he padded softly out of the mosque with the manuscript, the new Manuscript of Belz, wrapped in a kerchief in his valise. He slipped down the hill and splashed out onto the road, ignored by the dogs who yawned and shook off the rain as he passed.*

That very same night, of course, the tanks and armored trucks of the Interior Police had climbed the hills on the outskirts of Belz. They paused now among the walnut trees on the edge of town. Young men with shaven heads and blue eyes passed the hours smoking furtively and watching the lights of Belz flicker in the rain. They were eager for the sun to come up and their work to begin, for fighters from the hills had struck hard in the capital city, and the soldiers knew what revenge they would seek in the damp town below them.

As the sun rose, the soldiers swiveled their rockets and fired at the mosque. The shells slammed into its walls, shaking them shrilly, clapping them like bells. Thick smoke poured from the white rock walls. The soldiers rushed into town with the tanks close behind. They gathered Belz men, still bleary-eyed from sleep, and began sorting them out. Any man with rough hands and tanned skin they judged a fighter; they pushed these men against walls and shot them in their faces. The councilor who had argued appeasement now tottered bareheaded from his house, offering bread and salt in his raised hands. A soldier hit him in the head with the butt of his rifle. Soldiers caught women hiding in root cellars and raped them. They burned the low silos and they shot the milk cows while the stones of the mosque rolled and cracked in the flames that incinerated the famous manuscript and the old man, who died asleep in his cell. As sour smoke curled among the piles of rubble, soldiers laughed and took turns firing across the fields at townspeople running into the walnut orchards. Those running through the fields did not notice how the sun, rising for once in a clear sky, had warmed the dew in the grass.

The soldiers caught Fadim as they were driving out of the uprooted town. He had hidden in a bank of grass along the road where the rocket tanks had stopped, and had been too frightened to move. As the tanks churned through the ditches and over the road one made straight for him, *forcing him to run, and the soldiers pointed their rifles at his head. A young soldier, deprived of spoils by his comrades, demanded that Fadim give up his valise. Convinced by his pallor and the softness of his hands that he was no fighter from the hills, the soldiers told him to go away. As they drove Fadim off with taunts and blows, the young soldier prised open the case, spilled its contents into the mud, and cursed to find nothing of value.*

TIME CAPSULES

For reasons too trivial to relate, I find myself basking in the yellow pixelation of a mercury-vapor streetlamp on a cold night in mid-November. What skein of events, what arrangement of acts and things led me to this moment? The catalogue of causes is endless and banal: boredom with cello and the chess-prodigy circuit; ruin of college and serial gaming obsessions; pressure of graduate school, dwindling prospects of success . . . the keening of flocks of returning geese as they hurtle through the darkness overhead mingles with a fresh-conjured headache to make me wistful and retrospective. But this kind of thinking has become all but incomprehensible to me now. It's simpler to focus on the physiology: a drop in cystolic dopamine levels in synaptic clefts, the surging reuptake of serotonin permitting withdrawal's early tidal seepage, a trickle of psychic acid already ravaging holes in my levees. So here I stand beneath a ceiling of goose-honk waiting for a car to turn the corner and fleetingly toggle its headlights, at which signal I'll slip into the curbside shadows to commit a violation of Schedule II of the Controlled Substances Act.

But as the car makes its wonted turn, a rustle from behind raises my nape-hairs. I wheel and confront a hectic silhouette, epaulets and porkpie hat.

"D'ye know me Simon Moyes?" he asks in a too-loud voice.

"Why no, I . . . "

The awaited car speeds up, gliding away to my left. I watch it recede, then turn to the interloper.

"I'm sure we've never met. If you'll excuse me . . . "

"These are yours," he says, and thrusts a bag at my face.

Bewildered, I take the bag and walk away at a furious pace without looking back. This isn't the way it usually happens. But I'm curious—and I'm sweating, and my brain is trying to throb its way free. So I open the jar, shake one of the strangely heavy pills into my palm. I lick, registering some shock as the pad of my tongue goes utterly numb at the pressure of the pill. Not tingly-numb—void-numb. And then I swallow, the same curious sensation following the pills' passage down my trachea and through my abdomen, like some dark searchlight revealing caverns in my body, splintering abysses.

And then that sensation explodes.

I am hunched, looking down and forward, and I feel myself begin to stretch out ahead. The world peels away from a me that is not me, absenting itself by degrees in some shimmering granularity, the *what-am-I-now* caterpillaring through unblinking moments as I fall back and back, a back which is also a down—and everything goes away from me, the shadowed trees, the road in all its particles, all of it now extruding at every point as a taffy-rope of time wide as the world dangles me, bobs me backwards, holds me skidding in place while the stream rushes on. And then the whole of self settles back into self, back into a moment which endures and dies like all the others ever have, and something like a sense of now restores itself by degrees through all my corpuscles.

I'm back in the pool of piss-light, where I stand shivering. A car peels around the corner. A cool blade of saliva lies against my chin. The car's headlights flicker familiarly. And then a rustle behind me stirs my nape.

Comes the voice again: "D'ye know me Simon Moyes?" Croaking, exhortatory, like an Ahab of indolence.

I turn as I had before, but now I only gape dumbly. Staggering away, into the light and out of it again, I slip in dry gravel. At the crunch of road-matter I notice that the geese are gone—their honk silenced, their low-hurtling palpability now an absence in the sky. And the fellow in the porkpie and the epaulets still stands at the edge of the light; I make my way up the gentle hill back to the bus stop and as I turn the corner I look back down the street and still he's there.

I feel as if I've climbed out of a pit of déjà vu—a flash of recurrence that registers not in the forebrain, but behind the heart, in kidneys and knees, down to the tingling jointures of toe and nail. An estranged exhilaration overtakes me, an uncanny renewal, as if standing at the window of some grim teller I had just redeemed a fistful of misspent moments.

At home I tear the unmarked glass jar out of the bag and shake out a few capsules, which jiggle to rest on the scuffed countertop. One rolls under the door of the microwave, whose clock with its blinking dots reminds me of the lateness of the hour: a quarter to midnight. The moon has risen, filling a pane of the kitchen window. Retrieving the pill from the nook and holding it up in the light, I take note for the first time of its mottled translucence, an opaline swirl like the atmosphere of some unknown planet, at once prismatic and black. Or our own planet; the whorls now figure white and pale blue. But here an unexpected something I notice—it moves. Whatever compound the capsules contain is swirling, motile, a flickering cloudscape in fisheye miniature.

These are not the sort of pills to which I am accustomed. In fact I've never used anything like them. By some obscure action they accomplished a reset of my withdrawal, which I had not even noticed until I stepped off the bus and walked to my building. Only now am I beginning to feel the need edging its way into the scene again, clouding my cup of consciousness. But of the business with the return of the fellow with hat and coat, and the rehearsal of our script of a minute before, I can only wonder.

Refreshed by curiosity, I pop the pill into my mouth. Like the first, this one takes its numbing, abyssal course; again there is the soul-dangling sensation of the world leaving me behind. But having anticipated it I find it voluptuous, empowering, lightening. It takes its course out of time; I don't know how long I stand there shivering in the flux. But suddenly—with no leaking let-down, but a sudden phase shift—I'm here again, feeling my pulse in my palms as I press them to the counter. And then I notice the microwave clock beating its lucent tattoo, only with a difference: it now reads 11:44.

I've learned to trust anything but the fickle essay of my senses. And so, I pop another pill: the delicious absence, the dangle in the gyre. And when I come to a rest again, the clock reads 11:43. I pop five more; the house flings apart and reassembles itself five minutes earlier. Tears are puddling in my eyes, spidering the digits: 11:38. But for their crimson glow the room is utterly black; the moon is gone. Perhaps it is behind a cloud, waiting to reappear at 11:44? Aside from this unexpected change, I feel completely well. Beyond a fleeting dizziness there is no discernible down—no cotton-mouth thirst, no headache, no hunger.

The next day I take the train into town. Often I go there to watch the chess-players in the square—rarely to play; the game's heights long ago proved too giddy for me. My game-playing propensities find their outlet now online. To be sure, I never play the shambling prince of the plaza: the fellow in the straw hat whose little sign, depending from the table, pronounces him the "Chess Master," who entertains tourists with feats of ludic legerdemain. (Candidly, I will admit that I played him once while my postgraduate career was in steep decline. But I couldn't unseat the old liar, who sits there still in his incongruity like a polo player with a tattoo.)

Today I stroll and sit at intervals, wondering what to do with the time capsules. Of course I could use them to get rich, or at least to engage in some significant larceny: watch the lottery announcement while standing in a convenience store, then pop a pill, pick the numbers, and cash in. I could save them for emergencies—in case of injury or the onset of illness. I could use them to make a hero of myself, backing up to just before the emergent moment to thwart the cause: to pull the child back from path of the oncoming truck, to turn trip the hold-up man before he begins his assault. It's an easy route to the kind of attention I crave—which means, of course, that it's only a criminal enterprise of another kind.

But what if the pills aren't the "time capsules" I think they are? It could easily be a delusion, the effect of a heretofore unknown but perfectly normative province of the pharmacopeia. What if time itself is a series of lottery-tumbles, each moment fixing a possibility plucked from the random flux? But even if it's so, maybe randomness opens up a window on the unlimited—maybe there's freedom in the swerve. I don't know. And now I realize that I'm becoming paranoid about the functioning of time itself, treating it as a kind of cosmic conspiracy.

Unsettled, I flow with the crowds of jobbers crossing the streets of the square at the lights. Drawn by force of habit, I find myself back at chess tables in the plaza by the cafe. And it occurs to me that here's a test to consider.

It occurs to me now what a great advantage the capsules could give me. The sixty-four squares, the thirty-two pieces, the two players—even with its millions of moves, the game offers a system in which these retrancheings of time might be modulated and controlled.

I watch the chess master dispense with a few comers before I take my chance. He beckons; I settle into the concrete dish of the chair, feeling the play across my face of the shadows of ash trees toiling in the breeze. The chess master is setting the black pieces in place when he peers up from beneath the weave of his straw hat. "Five minutes," he croaks, fiddling with two-faced chess clock at the edge of the board. His rheumy eyes swivel to glimmer up at me, pale balls of lightning caught in a well. I set the pieces in place on the terrazzo tabletop; the chess master still eyes me through the haze. I look down, move my queen's knight's pawn forward a single square and swipe the clock.

The chess master mirrors my move. He asks my name, and I tell him. Four moves follow in quick succession as we castle our respective kings. And then I realize an error: developing my king's bishop, I carry the move too far down the diagonal, leaving my position exposed. The bottle of pills is resting in my right hand; now I twist it open and pop one into my mouth.

And as I make this swift movement, and just before I tumble out of time, the chess master breaks into a smile.

I fix on the clock dials spinning back in the rattling aurora. When the world settles again, the board is set up before my mistaken move. I shift the bishop again, shortening by three squares the distance traveled. But soon enough I'm in trouble once more. This time I draw the bottle to the tabletop. Placing it on the board with a quiet clack, I dip out a capsule and hold its swirling iridescence up for the chess master's inspection.

"You've seen these before?"

Again, the smile, the reptile gleam in the orbits, as he draws from his vest pocket a grimy rubber coin purse, pinches open its mouth, takes out an identical pill.

We swallow simultaneously, and the battle is on. He comes out of the drop quicker than I do every time, making his moves as swiftly, grinning like a coyote battened on innocence. We're careening through time move by move, the chess clock teetering on the brink of five minutes. How much time passes for us I do not know, but I am learning the game's deeper twists and turns swiftly as we navigate the all-but-endless iterations. It's like I'm falling out of the sky into a hole in the earth: a familiar topography of gambits and defenses gives way to layers of estranged possibility. The figures of the lurkers and the chess-watchers shuttle in and out of the haze as our material conditions flutter and change: one moment we're shifting our pieces in the midst of a hail storm, then we find ourselves sitting in alone in a vast field of torn plastic, fires decorating the horizon. But in the precinct of the table nothing changes—our attire remains the same, the grit and stains of the chessboard keep their shapes and textures, even the ash tree still sways overhead.

And still we're only tearing at the late edges of the opening gambit. Looking into the bottle with a capsule poised at my lips, I notice that their number is greatly reduced. It took much longer than I expected to consume this many pills; it's as if they've been replenishing themselves. But now their number is dwindling.

"Look around," the chess master suddenly croaks. "It's getting gray."

Surveying the square, I notice how the light fails at a certain circumference, that beyond the limit of the plaza with its trees, all is cloudy absence.

"Maybe you ought to walk around a little, see what you can see."

I move away, noticing now how my knees creak as I stand. My body is tired, desiccated, crumbling. I walk away until the chess master and the trees recede in a pool of dim light. And then I return.

"Well, what's out there?" he asks.

"Nothing. Beyond the edge of sight there is nothing, nothing at all."

"Nothing, then?" he replies. "It's been going that way a long time now."

And suddenly it's clear. My first pill shut out the geese, locked their migration out of my time-bounded world. My binge in the kitchen cost me the moon. By some terrible relativity, gaining a moment of time causes the annihilation of some volume of space. Freedom in the swerve? I thought that's what the pills were about. But there is none of it, not for us addicts. Although my every urge would defy it, this is a universe in which nothing can be gained without cost. The existential economy may seem vast: order and entropy, matter and energy, space and time. But for all those abstractions, it's quite simple. And time is especially costly in our world, is it not?

It has grown chilly in this—this what, this move, this instantiation, this world . . . however I define our narrowing space, it has grown chilly, and a breeze still toils in the boughs of the ash tree. The chess master shivers. Reaching down to the great bag at his feet, he draws out a soiled trench coat by the epaulets.

I'm staggered with the recognition. "You," I say. "You're the one who came to me. You gave me the pills."

"Did I?" he replied, settling the coat about his shoulders. "Maybe I did. I remember a time, ages ago seems like, when I wanted to bolt from this place—this time, if you take my meaning. I thought of trying to sell the pills. Some version of me must've done it then, back in that other time."

"But why?" I ask.

"I can't say for sure," he replies. "Probably I figured you'd be the one to take my place. But I've lost track of that. Fork in the road came up, and I took it—took another pill, fought my way out of yet another game. But it only led to other games, and others, and others. And now I've lost track of the paths," he concludes, settling back in his seat. "As have you, I might add. I know that playing this way—taking the pills, drifting in the streams of time—I became 'the Chess Master.' Biding my time, so to speak, taking a pill whenever I made a bad move. I learned my way around the maze of the game, eventually."

I sit astonished. "And now you're lost in it," I stammer. "And so am I. In *this* time—and all the ones left to us, I guess—we're marooned, cut off."

At this the chess master only shrugs, holds up the capsule still caught in his fingertips, and regards me questioningly. "I don't know," he says. "But let's play on, what do you say?"

I look at game clock. The hand on my dial continues to move; I've nearly used up my limit of time. "Not yet," I say.

"Good for you," he replies. "Me, I've been doing this too long. Now I just want to go away—and when the pills run out, I wager, my time will be all spent up. But maybe you can take comfort in this: in one of the worlds we spawned, *you* are now the chess master. In another, storms of fire and sand and, who knows, maybe shredded plastic, have blown us both to bits. In one we're famous; in another we got dragged off to jail. And somewhere in there, you stepped away from the game early enough to find your way back." And with that, the chess master takes his pill. There is a momentary blur about his figure, too brief for casual notice. And there he sits still, pill tipped to lips.

I'm weeping. "I'm glad we took the time to talk about it, anyway," I say to the only other person I know. And looking now at the board, I see a move. It leads to check, but not to mate. I make the move, swipe the clock, swallow the pill. And once more the world falls away—now languidly, casually, fittingly—as it will again and again in a recession of timeworlds ever more intimate.

CAMERA LUCIDA

My middle-aged memories of the house by the sea, like the photographs my family took there, are caught up in the frothy state of betwixt-and-between that gave the place its grain: sharp grass and velvet mud, rush of water and crunch of shell, placid exteriors and rough-planked rooms. The images are vivid to me now, but their meaning is hidden, flickering and uncertain, boxed up and piled in shadows.

My father's great-grandfather had purchased the house by the sea around the turn of the last century, and it had been the scene of many family holidays down to my father's childhood. In the decades preceding my birth, however, a series of disputes among brothers and brides had set the place off-limits for a generation. My father had spent summers there as a child, but through college and engineering school and the early years of his marriage only fleeting visits had been possible; by the time I was born, the place was shunned by all sides of the family. But then some uncle unknown to me had died; some sort of resolution had been offered or fallen into, and that winter my cousins and I had heard our parents judiciously scheduling various visits over the phone.

Our turn came in late July, bringing hope of a respite from struggles within our household and without. The fraternals and collaterals of my father's side were not the only contested realm in our family; my parents, too, had skirmished often in the last few months, a running battle that seemed to wax and wane with every change in fortune. What could I do to change the tide? I was twelve years old, and both of them were perfect in every conceivable way. If my father could not keep his job, it must have been part of some tremendous design, the chief elements and ends of which lay outside my narrow borders. If my mother were drinking rather heavily —if the streaked and reeking pitcher she carried to breakfast and dinner always seemed too full, and to slop too often as she poured her glass—it must have been a necessary salve. And their faces grew fond whenever we talked about the house by the sea. Their memories of it were happy, their expectations of a salutary return too bright and hungry to brook any doubt.

We drove up mid-week, my mother preferring to miss a couple of days to avoid the weekend highway. I sat wedged sweatily between bocce and badminton sets, amidst suitcases, boxes of books, and pantry goods, while the road effected its slow reduction from multi-lane tollway to rolling blacktop to washed-out, sandy way snaking through scrub oak and huckleberries. The place itself sat on a low rise of windswept grass sheltered by broad sycamores, offering a stately contrast to the low, fey thatch of leather-leafed oaks. The tall pile of white clapboard and slate-gray porches looked slightly out of place, as if a suburban colonial had hitched up its skirts and tripped barefoot through the scrub to settle here before a swerve of sea.

And what a swerve it was—twelve feet beyond the back porch step, the windswept lawn gave way to a low, broken fieldstone wall at which the tidal current lapped. Beyond that landfall spread a sweep of water rippling its way amidst tussock-topped islands, a puzzle of beguiling insularities scattered a mile or more out to where the mud dropped away and the proper sea stood behind its shattering pale of surf. Close by the fieldstone break, a small sailboat lay hauled out on a hump of long grass, its sail and rigging furled and wound like some forgotten aegis. With the sun riding high amidst a tumult of clouds, the flats alive with a tapestry of wind-woven water to robe the granite beaches' whitened bones, the picture thus presented was a fair and memorable one.

By the time the last box was deposited on the kitchen table and the car doors finally closed, however, this scene had rearranged itself entirely. The tide having run out, the seascape was now a ruin of runneled mud and shellheap. Here and there lay mirrored pools of water like lozenges. People ranged across the distances of the newborn strand; in a couple of place boats lay stranded on their gunwales. I stumbled out to the edge of the grass and uttered a cry of astonishment.

"The tides run here like no place else," my mother called to me, settling into a chair on the porch with a heap of napkins for folding. "That's the quality of this stretch of coast," she continued, her bob of black hair bristling in the wind. "You come to visit one place, and turn around to find yourself in another."

"You've been here before?" I asked.

"When daddy and I first met," she replied, nodding. Referring to my father she used "daddy," a habit of her own family away down South, which to me always sounded strange.

49

"How was it then?" I asked.

She exhaled a long time. "The picture it presents today," she replied at last, "is utterly different."

I wondered what she could mean, but she only told me to run along and see what I might find on the mud flats. So I ventured out, straying far out among pools and rippled sands, climbing onto islands parked on the flats like feral ships run aground. I thrilled to the quiet implacable quality of time on the flats—the water trickling in almost imperceptibly as the islands' shadows stole across the sand—and especially the esoteric sense of being somewhere that wasn't. An hour before, these trackless, well-packed rills and dunes had been seafloor; in the space of six hours, they would be hidden again by waters. It was as if two wholly different places existed in one frame, diurnally revealed as the moon swept round the earth. Only the occasional holler or crash of wood from the old house on the rise reminded me of enduring reality.

That evening my father and I sat in the yellow glow of lamps as the moist cool stole in at the windows. The house's interior belied its stolid exterior—within, it looked like a circus tent woven together of unfinished planks. It had a roughhewn feel, but for the bookshelves lining nearly every wall with their ancient, salt-rimed sets of Harvard Classics and Blue-and-Gold Ticknor novels leaning softly into one another. My father sat with one of these books flopped open in his lap while I scooted about on my knees testing the drawers and cupboards. Off in the beadboard-lined kitchen, my mother was washing the dishes with infinite care, setting down plate after glass in a soft, moist, syncopated rhythm.

"You're unlikely to find anything of interest in the cupboards," my father intoned. "It's not as if we're the first to visit this place in any long while. Uncle Neal and his kids were here for the last three weeks, and my cousins have been coming for years unabated. Those ruffians have likely ransacked the place for trinkets by now."

He wasn't quite right. I had managed to find a few prizes: a greasy bottle of tanning lotion, a frosty pill of beach glass, a tiny troll doll that looked as if had been chewed upon. I was about to give up when I found—not in a drawer, but in a kind of hinged magazine rack nestled behind the lampstand—a camera. And a marvelous camera at that: a black, steel-lipped scallop-shell of leather, which popped open to reveal a lens retracted into a kind of bed of bellows, set in a face of polished chrome beneath a plate of lensed plastic.

"Let's see," said my father, taking the camera in his large red hands and pudging up his face as he turned it over. He explained that it was an old Land camera, an old style of Polaroid, which took pictures on instant film that developed, with the application of a chemical squeegee inserted into a pocket in the camera's shell, in about a minute's time.

"It says it's got film in it," he said, pointing at a tiny fogged window with the number "7" framed within. I asked if I could take a picture with it, to see if it worked. "Well I don't see why not," he replied, dropping his book and grinning wanly as I aimed the camera at him. I pressed the cool back to my face—there was a smell of rust and old leather that seemed to carry me to faraway places—my finger fumbled for the shutter button, and the whole machine shuddered a moment before a plane of photo paper came flicking out like a tongue, emitting a clean, alkaline smell that blended pleasingly with the former mustiness.

"Now take it out," he said, nodding at the dangling photo. I did, and he showed me how to withdraw the squeegee from its little scabbard to drag a foul blue gel across the photo's milky emulsion. "Set it here," he said, indicating the broken-edged marble table top next to his armchair. I laid it down gently, as if it were made of glass, and we both leaned over it as the image resolved by uncanny, slow degrees.

And after a breathless moment, there it was: a photographic image. But not of my father, not of the armchair, not of any scene offered in the house by the sea. Instead we saw a sunlit pagoda at the end of a red-railed bridge nestled amidst blossom-heavy boughs.

We stared at the photograph a moment, and then our eyes met. I asked my father if the picture could have been taken by someone else and jammed in the mechanism until we released it. "It doesn't work that way," he replied, shaking his head uncertainly and reaching for the camera. He handled it a moment like a broken thing, turning it over soft-handedly as if it were an injured bird. Then quickly he aimed the lens at me—I smiled reflexively—and pressed the shutter button. The mechanism wheezed; a new photograph protruded, its imagery still veiled. Treated and set upon the table, its streaked surface slowly dried and brightened to reveal a woman standing between railroad tracks in shorts and fluffy bedroom slippers, her face turned from view.

His face screwed up in fretful curiosity, my father got up and strode about the room, taking three pictures in rapid fire. He aimed at the ceiling, the floor, and the door to the kitchen; a disappointed-looking pier, a collapsed hot-air balloon, and a white Labrador retriever with its leash in its mouth, resolved in turn before our eyes.

My mother stole in behind us as we looked at the images on the chipped marble. "Where'd you find those?" She asked.

My father stood upright, aimed the camera, and snapped, my mother presenting an instant rictus of flashbulb smile. He yanked the photo from the camera, squeegeed it, and handed it over. Her smile dissolved as she watched the image appear. She showed it to us: newly-pollarded trees marching along a road; tall, leafless elms on a smudged horizon. The next morning, my father drove into town looking for a place that carried the right kind of film, while my mother sat at the long dining table and looked over the photographs made by the camera. She was shuffling them before her as if they were a game of solitaire.

I asked what she was looking for, but she didn't want to talk. "Did you have your breakfast?" she asked. "Then why not go for a sail?" she continued at my nodding reply.

"The tide is coming in."

Though her faraway tone made me curious, I wordlessly complied. As she was occupied with the photographs, I slipped the camera from its place on the lampstand and took it along. The little window indicated there was one shot left, and we had no replacement film as yet. But I wanted to discover what I would find the next time I pushed the shutter button.

I had learned to sail in summer camp, and although the boat was new to me it readily disclosed its secrets. On the grassy bank by the water I stepped the mast and unfurled the sail. Laying the camera carefully in the little forward cuddy cabin, I pushed the boat into the turbid water, tucked into the cockpit, and set a long reach across an elbow of tidal current where it bent to cradle the nearest island.

I sailed a long while in that uncentered labyrinth, the white pile of the house dipping and hiding as I tacked amidst the bars and islands hemmed in by the far-off surge of surf. I only turned back when the centerboard began scraping the sand as the tide ran out. Heading homeward, I stopped on the near island and removed the camera from the latched cuddy. Standing on the shore, I quickly aimed at the house and snapped a photo. When the image at last appeared, it showed the house as I was looking at it, with—and this I had not noticed while taking the picture—my father standing amidst the long grass by the water with his hands upraised. I looked up across and there he stood, still waving, his shouts a rumor on the water. I waved the oddly accurate photograph at him as if he should see it over the distance and then quickly shoved off for home.

He was furious. "You took the camera?" he spluttered.

"I didn't know I shouldn't," I replied.

"It's special!" he shouted. "It's very special—very special. It shouldn't be taken out of the house."

I turned the photograph over to him. He looked up and gazed across the outflowing water to the island as if to make sure it was there.

"A very special camera," he mumbled, turning and walking up the grass. Flicking a look back over his shoulder, he said, "bring it now."

But we did take it out of the house, and soon. Over the next few days it was our family's entire business to investigate the ways of the camera. We had already discovered that beyond the house it took pictures of the scene it was presented with; only inside did it reveal other locales and unknown persons. One day we took the camera with us on a drive to the village nearby, shooting entirely conventional pictures of ourselves seated on stone walls or eating fried clams by the harbor. It occurred to my mother that perhaps the photographs we took while away from the house might be shared with some other camera in some other place. She brought along a small dry-erase board from the kitchen to hold in front of ourselves whenever we took a picture, thus to furnish unknown (and perhaps nonexistent) others with dates, places, and names. In this way our family photographs took on the quality of messages in bottles—although we flung them into an abyss, a sea we never could see. But there were: me with fudgesicle and flip-flops, my father's white t-shirt luminous, my mother's jacket collar popped against the sea-summer chill, all of us floating to the surface on our estranged smiles.

Indoors each night we clicked away, amassing an inventory of enigmas. I still remember many of the photographs, though I no longer have them to hand: a sumptuous spiral staircase, its banisters of dark wood, its treads clad in rich red carpet; a hand-cranked ice cream maker streaming with meltwater; the artfully-framed boughs of an aged oak from which peered the eyes of what looked like a dog, but must have been some forest creature. Rarely did the photographs depict people; when they did, their faces were turned away or veiled. Unlike our own photographs, in which we grinned foolishly around our scrawled-upon sign. This discrepancy made me wonder whether we had guessed the camera's workings correctly; but my parents never remarked upon it, and as with many other mysteries I kept my own counsel.

As these days and nights passed in the house by the sea, a change came over my parents. Each had latched onto an obsession: for my father, the camera's mechanism became the object of all his intent. Numerous times he dismantled the machinery with great care, holding the tiny, flashing parts up to the lamplight and examining them minutely. I would find him rummaging in the closets, peering into the attic, splintering back loose floorboards as he hunted in vain for some explanatory circuitry embedded in the very timbers of the house. My mother, meanwhile, each night arranged and rearranged our growing deck of exotica, seeking patterns in the tumult of imagery. Some nights she attempted a geographical sorting, although the locations proved too uncertain to venture guesses upon. She placed them into two rows, one with people and one without; the animals she first counted with the people, then shook her head and slid them one by one to the unpopulated side. She smoked as she worked, wreathing her short hair, her spectacles, and her fruitless cartomancy in glamorous rings and clouds. She played any number of suits and tricks: wild and domestic animals, urban scenes and rural, indoors and out, marine and terrestrial; even the colors obsessed her. But as her ashtray filled, these shufflings disclosed no distinct meaning to her ever-reddening eyes.

At night, shouts and thumps from the upstairs bedroom continued unabated. I was not unaccustomed to such night sounds, and yet as the camera worked its way into our family life they took on a fresh vehemence. One night—the air heavy and still, the beam from a faraway lighthouse flickering as it searched the muslin curtains—I climbed the stairs and stood in their bedroom doorway. Shadows reared and loomed as my parents stalked and shouted and the ceiling fan spun on its stalk. "Can't we put things back together?" my father pleaded. "We can put things back together."

"You can take it apart and put it back together any which way," mother replied. "You're good at that, aren't you? Always putting things together and taking them apart. But it doesn't change anything. It'll work the same no matter how you put it together. It's the nature of it to do what it does to us."

I thought they were talking about the camera. When they looked at me, I asked them what was wrong, whether it was the camera, what we could do to fix it. My mother came to me, sweaty and wet-cheeked; soap and ashes enfolded me as she took me in her arms, saying, "and here he is, our little picture. Only he's no self-portrait, is he? He's something else altogether. Where did he come from? Where did you come from, little picture?" She took me back to my bed and stayed with me, crooning that refrain—"where did you come from, little picture"—until I fell asleep.

When I awoke the next morning, she was gone—back to the city, my father said. We returned ourselves in a couple of days, me sitting in the front seat. He dropped me off at home and left to stay with friends in the next town over. When mother went away—some months later, after my father had returned home—she took with her the photographs we made at the house by the sea. I supposed that she was looking for the places we had glimpsed in them, hoping to stitch them together. It was a solace that she took both the images of ourselves and the mysteries together in one small box. But I never learned whether she found a sorting to make the photographs yield their story.

We went to the place the next July, daddy and I, but my father wanted nothing to do with the camera. He dismantled it one last time, put the pieces in the drawer, and never spoke of it again. We frittered away the month generously sailing the inlets and sounds, picking rocks and shells on the flats, fishing or watching the stars wheeling in the night. A few times my father would turn in early, and I would sneak into the parlor to examine the disassembled camera. In subsequent summers I tried the puzzle of the parts until I made the camera whole again. And then—for by then I was going alone to the house by the sea—I started taking pictures. Only my object had changed: now I was hoping for an image that might show mother to me. I consumed many packets of film, discovered many images of unknown people, places, and things. Finally, the manufacturer stopped making film stock for the camera and the flow of cryptic images ceased. Looking through pictures of unknown dogs and uneaten wedding cakes, perfectly-set tables and unkempt lawns, only one image provokes my curiosity. In it, a woman looks across a street as if making ready to cross, or maybe she's waiting for someone. She wears a quilted jacket, its collar popped familiarly; her bob of black hair seems to bristle as she steps away.

FOR PROVISIONAL DESCRIPTION OF
SUPERFICIAL FEATURES

The surface of the OGLE-350c, like so many other superearths Sevin and Vulpes had visited, was composed of a mixture of crumbly xenolith and light, rubbery, frozen organics mounded like ice cream—if ice cream were ever black, and piled into geologic deposits that stood weathering in a thin corrosive atmosphere for ten million years. Here and there great cavities yawned in the frozen matrix, dark and questioning. In the distance, perhaps a kilometer away, a long sharp ridge carved into the crepuscular sky, its edge shining spectacularly pink where it caught the light of OGLE-350c's sun. But that was well out of range, beyond the anti-radiation field thrown out by the lander.

"It's quite a feature," Vulpes said. "We should try to reach it on our next trip down."

Sevin turned from the view of the distant ridge, looking back towards Vulpes and the lander beyond. "I'm beginning my survey," he said.

"Fine," Vulpes replied. "I'll start looking for a place to deploy the density probe."

They were well matched, Sevin and Vulpes—but nothing less was expected of exploration agents, whose complementary dispositions were artfully chosen and groomed. Where Vulpes was credulous and eager, Sevin was skeptical and high-strung. But these are crude names for the subtly mutual sets of skills and tendencies the two possessed; and their carefully modulated qualities, augmented with judicious neuronal and glandular enhancements, had seen them efficiently from one strange world to another over the long, seasonless years of their mission.

With Vulpes lost to sight, Sevin cranked his helmeted head back and stared into the luminous sky, as if he could see in its stationary orbit the ship that had carried them through wormholes and storms of dark matter to half a dozen worlds before OGLE-350c. But musing on tenuous connections strayed beyond the protocols of his training. Sevin's mind snapped back to the task at hand, busying himself with click-tagging the geomorphology of various features. It was a simple procedure, one that offered Sevin a too-placid target upon which to concentrate his mental energies. The recorder did all of the work, syncing the measured coordinates with the networked map in the ship's system seven hundred kilometers above his head. He tried putting aside the mind-numbing cascades of decisions that awaited in the form of search protocols and the dizzying strangeness of the new world itself, but to little avail. He and Vulpes would be on-world three days, until the energy core supplying power to the anti-radiation field was depleted and could be charged no more. Only then would they head back to orbit for a resupply and a few hours of blissful suspension. Then the next mission site would be selected, and they would descend again.

Clicking away with the recorder, Sevin was soon lost in reverie: concentrating on outcrops of xenolith, his mind wandered back through the nebulae, past the torrential labyrinths of energy pouring into black holes and the deadly jets of pulsars, and beyond these things back to Earth and its bacterial seas burping and sloughing in the heat. He was moving along slowly, tagging and pondering, when Vulpes' voice crackled over the link.

"You've got to come see this," Vulpes said in an uncanny tone.

"What have you got?" Sevin asked. "A notable feature?"

"No," Vulpes coughed. "Or, yes. It's something else. Really something else. You're not going to believe it."

Sevin waved his hand across his faceplate to activate the heads-up. "I've got your position and I'm coming to you now."

"There is a screen," Vulpes said, muttering over the link. "And, ah . . . there are keys."

"What was that?" Sevin replied.

"They've got Internet," Vulpes said.

Vulpes' icon flickered on the augment screen of Sevin's visor, winking and throbbing among the outlines of burly outcrops of xenolith. Sevin fought his urge to hurry, maintaining a measured pace, remembering to *observe, record, reflect,* as the protocols admonished. He soon found himself standing before a cavernous opening, a rounded mouth in the xenolith hung with deliquescent methane salts. It was a harrowing prospect, clambering into that maw, and yet Vulpes had done it—even now his icon flashed slightly to the left where, to Sevin's eyes, there was only a wall of irredeemable rock. He smiled—Vulpes' placid courage was a benefit, even if his rushed judgments could prove less useful. And now he saw flickering-in the hole the unmistakable icy blue of Vulpes' light diode.

The passage sloped gently downward and made a sharp left turn, then a right. Sevin crouched slightly to enter the chamber that now glowed with Vulpes' diode. The room was not large, although its ceiling was high. It presented a nearly-incomprehensible sight: the walls and floor seemed fashioned, almost hewn, from the dead rock with rough linearity—but rose upwards into a twisting kind of narrow dome, almost as if the room had been held aloft by some giant hand and spun while the rock was still hot and taffy-soft. From the lower ramparts of this dizzying ceiling, great loops or coils of rock depended, their filaments the thickness of an arm, reaching almost to the floor. Near the far wall stood a desk—it could only be called a desk—upon which sat a pedimented flat panel that bathed Vulpes' visor with its light. It was this in fact, and not his diode, that lit the room. The many-legged density probe lay upon the floor behind him, undeployed.

Vulpes was staring at the screen and tapping at keys arrayed on neatly on a long tablet—a keyboard—lying on the desk before him. Since the emergence of Ubiquity around 2100, there had been little use for screens and keys—when everything is effectively a screen *in potentia*, nothing needs to be a screen in fact. And so sets like the one on the desk were quaint—still useful, like transistor radios in the early 2000s; rare, but not exactly collectible. Most had been ground by disuse and abandonment to the plastic dust, or "flash," that glutted the seashores and sometimes rose in great storms lit by static charges. But the set here looked less like a keepsake or remembrance of human history than an artifact of alien rumor, a notion of a computer forged or fashioned or spat out by something that heard of, but never seen, a real 21st century computer beneath the gray skies of Earth.

"You have got to check this out." Vulpes' voice, crackling over the link.

Sevin stood there pondering him, listening to the air-handling units whirr deep in his suit. And then he smiled. "How did you manage it?" he asked.

Vulpes looked up. The screen's bright prism hung in front of his face, caught in the resin of his visor. "What do you mean?" he asked.

"You pulled a fast one on me there. Secreting an old-school computer on the mission. Where did you stow it? It's too big for personal effects."

Vulpes pushed back his chair. *He was sitting in a chair.* "Friend," he said. "Take a look at this rig. It's like nothing I've ever seen, not even on the auctions."

Sevin crossed the room and stood next to Vulpes. The gear looked not molded, but extruded. There was something faintly geological about it, not unlike the deliquescent stalagmites that festooned the planet' surface.

"What's it made of?" Sevin asked.

"No clue," Vulpes replied. His gloved fingers had returned to the keys, but he reached up and tapped the bezel of the screen with a snap of his fingers. "Ceramic, maybe, or some sort of nanofiber matrix. Hold on, I'm gonna check my blips."

Sevin chuffed into his helmet and rolled his eyes. Social media at the center of the galaxy, twenty-four thousand light years from Earth! He watched Vulpes tapping the keys and squirming in his seat for a few seconds until he felt an urge to tear his helmet off. Fighting it down, he reasoned through grinding teeth. "Vulpes, look. This cannot be what you think it is."

Vulpes hissed. "Aw, blips aren't working. Must not be compatible with the ancient protocols on this machine—either that, or service is down."

"Can't be down," Sevin said. "How would your blips get here? The only conceivable source is Earth's orbital network, and that's electromagnetic. It travels at light speed, Vulpes. Think about it: 24,000 years ago there was no network of any kind to bleed off its transmissions into interstellar space."

"Not on Earth," Vulpes said.

"Not on Earth?"

"Right. I mean, what if it started off-world? What if it came from here?"

"You're suggesting that some kind of—of *Ogleans* crossed the Milky Way to build us an Internet?"

Vulpes' dark eyes glimmered wetly through his visor.

"Look around you," Sevin continued. "The planet's surface is composed predominantly of methane and xenolith, type unknown. Rads are metering 650 rem beyond the lander's field. Nothing lives here to make an Internet."

"We've been here three and a half hours, Sevin. One preliminary landing, one incomplete site survey. We don't have spectroscopy or exobiometry—we haven't even scoped the horizon yet. Is it just possible that we don't know everything about OGLE-350c?"

Sevin didn't have an answer. He stormed to the far wall, resistors cranking and torquing at his knees, and gave one of the loops of rock a smack.

"Hang on," Vulpes said. "They've got Wikipedia."

"Wiki—oh, come on." Sevin threw his hands up in a vague, gloved sign of parody. "The Ogleans and the making of Wikipedia!" he exclaimed.

For Sevin and Vulpes the name "Wikipedia" glowed with the aura of antiquity. It was a distant ancestor of the Ubiquity of their own time, the network of thoughts and things taking the form of congenitally curious botmobs hurling themselves about in the cyberspatial kaleidoscope—ever worrying, ever tweaking the fields and entries in those vast, intercalating, quasi-living datastorms that seethed behind Ubiquity's dappled surfaces. The powers and possibilities of Ubiquity made the device-bound Internet of old a creaky memory, suitable only for nostalgia salons and curiosity cabinets. But not even Ubiquity could reach here, these hundreds of parsecs from home.

Sevin watched Vulpes' eyes as they flitted greedily in the glow of the screen. "People used to complain about Wikipedia all the time," he said. "They accused it of systemic bias and inconsistencies, said that it favored consensus over credentials. It was a pretty crude tool."

"They also said it compared well to the accuracy of the old printed encyclopedias," Vulpes replied.

"That isn't saying very much," Sevin suggested.

Vulpes continued to stare at the screen and punch the keys. "Let's see if—oh, it's loading. Look, it's in here! Only hang on—"

"What?" Although he preferred not to, Sevin returned to Vulpes and peered over his shoulder.

"I looked up my name," Vulpes said, "and look what it has instead."

Sevin peered in at the screen and read:

Vulpes is a genus of the Canidae family, members of which share the common name "fox."

"I'm a fox, Sevin!" Vulpes exclaimed, laughing. "I've never seen one, of course. But that's my name, that's what it means."

"Shhh!" Sevin replied. "I'm reading." He leaned in closer. "It says they were smaller than dogs."

Both men were quiet a moment. "Go ahead," said Sevin, "look them up, too."

Vulpes fumbled over the keys for a moment and clicked. A new page of text popped into view, accompanied by a picture of a grassy expanse occupied by a blond, avuncular creature with dark eyes and a stout rope of a tail.

"A dog," Vulpes said. "And grass. Grass, and a dog."

"Never have seen one of those either," Sevin said, speaking for them both. The resistors sang in the legs of his suit as he shifted his weight.

Vulpes sat in front of the terminal, pecking with one finger and watching the screen. "Oh," he said after another moment, "This place is in here, too."

"What do you mean?" Sevin replied.

"OGLE-350c," Vulpes said. "They made an entry for it." And there it was—an antique encyclopedia entry for the planet they were standing on, flickering on the screen in dumb, plodding text with a few diagrams and pictures strewn about.

Sevin leaned in and read:

Physical characteristics

OGLE-350c orbits around its star at an average distance of 2.0 to 4.1 AU, or an orbit that would fall between the orbits of Mars and Jupiter in our own solar system. The variation in distance is the range of error in measurement and calculation; the planet's orbital elements are not known. Until this discovery, no small exoplanet had been found farther than 0.15 AUs from a main sequence star. The planet takes approximately 10 Earth years to orbit its star (located in the constellation

Scorpius), which is thought to be a cool red dwarf (95% probability), or a white dwarf (4% probability), with a very slight chance that it is a neutron star or black hole (<1% probability).

"Look at this," Vulpes hissed. "Check out what they knew about it."

Sevin pondered, his eyes narrowing. "Who?" he asked.

"People," Vulpes replied. "Us! Them! People in the olden days."

"And look what they didn't know," Sevin answered. "Nothing about the planet's orbit, nothing about its nature and composition or seismic activity. They didn't even know much about the star! Their means of exoplanetary detection were crude, remember—roughly speaking, they had the same technology used by Galileo."

"But there's more . . ."

"It doesn't matter!" Sevin cried. "What is it doing here? That's what matters. It's one hundred and forty-two degrees below zero, Vulpes. Screw your helmet back on and think. What is it doing here?"

"It says that this was the first small exoplanet discovered," Vulpes offered. "Maybe that's got something to do with this?"

"How so?"

"Maybe they knew their planet had been discovered, knew it was being watched."

"I don't see how that's possible," Sevin replied. "No, the only answer that makes any sense is this: another mission arrived before us and left this as some kind of bizarre calling card. Maybe it's an ansible, maybe some emulation technology we've never encountered. I'm sure if we look around a little, we'll figure out how they did it."

They searched for a power supply like the old systems had, but found none; nor could they find a way to turn the display off or to access other systems. They searched the chamber for an hour, Sevin tagging the whole place for later reconstruction. And all the while the screen lit the chamber, its blue light receding into the dim upper reaches of the high, twisted ceiling. But there was no indication of the source of the terminal, its power supply, or of the communications system that supplied it with data. After they had pursued their fruitless search for what seemed like an hour, Sevin announced that time was running out on the lander's anti-radiation field, and that they would need to return to the module while it recharged.

Later, Sevin tossed in his hammock inside the comfortably pressurized craft, pondering the words in the old Wikipedia entry. An orbit that would fall between the orbits of Mars and Jupiter . . . Until this discovery, no small exoplanet had been found. Somehow, the tissue of tentative declarations made him powerfully nostalgic for the home system: for Earth and its Moon nestled between the tidal eddies of Jupiter and the protective emissions of Sol, for warm green things he had never even seen. Since leaving he had witnessed the death of cold stars and the churning of nebulae as big as the solar system; he had slept in suspension through more years than there were generations between Wikipedia's age and his own. And now the time that had passed since that era seemed a shorter span than the reaches of space separating him from home. With these thoughts spinning in his head—with Earth's colors swimming in his mind's eye—he fell away into fitful sleep.

He awoke with a start some hours later, the airlock alarm pinging insistently and the cabin lights at full power. He rolled his head to the left; Vulpes' hammock was empty. Sevin leaped up and looked out the landing survey window to see his companion's helmeted figure making its bent way beyond the capsule's fuzzy shadow and into the field of excrudescences and outcrops nearby. Sevin had no doubt where he was headed.

He finished the tedious suiting procedures in half the usual time, clambered out of the airlock, and sped down the path now marked in the frozen lith by the scuttle of their boots. Already he had tried to raise Vulpes by the usual frequencies, to no avail. In the cavern now, he rounded the glimmering corner and entered the blue-lit chamber, where he found Vulpes in the appointed place, seated at the terminal. At first he feared the worst: Vulpes' arms hung at his sides, his body slumped slightly to one side. Sevin shook him, and was relieved when Vulpes' visored face shook and gazed up at him. "Look what it says," Vulpes stammered. "Look what it says—about us."

"Vulpes, let's get back to the lander now. The rad field isn't fully charged; it has got less than half an hour of power left in it."

"Just look!"

Sevin turned and read the entry:

Discovery

In 2201 CE, Corporation agents Sevin K. and Vulpes D. reached OGLE-350c. It was the fourth exoplanet of their tour of duty, which had begun at the superearth Centauri-f forty-two years before. There as elsewhere, they planned to spend several planetary missions making provisional descriptions of superficial features. Unfortunately it proved to be their last mission; the two agents never transmitted their ansible report from the OGLE system, and while electromagnetic telemetry later proved that they had established an orbit around OGLE-350c, they were never heard from again; cause of mission failure unknown.

He read it, and then he read it again, his fear climbing through the hairs along his spine. But in an instant fear became a kind of fierce clarity. "Let me in there," he said, pushing Vulpes' away.

Vulpes staggered. "What're you going to do?" he asked.

"People used to modify these entries," Sevin said.

"Who?"

"Anyone. Users." Sevin's eyes were darting, his fingers flexing. "Someone is making this up, and I'm going to unmake it."

"Really? You can change entries yourself?"

"The Internet wasn't like Ubiquity; it did what you told it to do."

Vulpes gulped audibly. "Seem like *it's* telling *us* what to do now."

But Sevin wasn't listening; he was intent on intuiting the workings of the system. He fumbled a few times before finding the edit field and setting the blinking line where he wanted text to enter. And slowly—punching the keys was hard enough with his gloved and unpracticed fingers—he began to enter text. "Sevin K. and Vulpes D. made their planetary EVA successfully and returned to their ship," he typed.

"There," he said. "A message for them." He clicked to go back out to the main page of the entry—and moaned as he read the new entry. Instead of "made" it read "failed to make"—different from before, but amounting to the same thing.

"Somebody is out to get us," Sevin said. "They've lured us here, it's clear enough. Someone's playing a game. It could be another mission—but no, how could that be? We'd know it, the system would've pinged us."

"Sevin," Vulpes said. "We've got to get away from here."

Sevin looked at the terminal through narrowed eyes. "I'm not done yet."

"But we're running out of time."

"I have to make them stop!" Sevin yelled. He had begun typing again; he had found the talk page, and was scanning for names and the timestamps of the edits.

Vulpes grabbed him by the wrist. Sevin's helmeted head swiveled towards him as his free hand jabbed out and smashed Vulpes in the chest. It wasn't a heavy blow, but Vulpes' resistors couldn't react quickly enough and he toppled heavily backwards, landing on his side.

"You had to come back out here," Sevin hissed. He could hear Vulpes breathing over the link. "And now I am going to fix this entry."

With that there was a squeal in both men's ears; the lander's anti-radiation field—all that was keeping them alive in this cosmically-blasted landscape—was running out of charge. The alarm signaling five minutes of power was driving itself insistently into their heads. Sevin fell back into the chair and set to the keys once more.

Vulpes watched him a full beat. "I'll go back and try to give it an emergency recharge," he said. And he left Sevin there to make his way back to the lander.

Upon his return Vulpes didn't pause to egress from his suit, but rushed to the field generator and stoked the manual recharger with a few dozen cranks of the handle. But that added only a few more seconds of power to the field. Invisibly, cosmic radiation flooded back into the area from every direction; now, only inside the lander was it safe. Sevin in the tapered chamber would have been protected but a few moments longer; by now his anger had been burned away.

Vulpes went to the outer bulkhead window and watched the

still landscape for some while, but Sevin never reappeared. He knew what he would find there, and knew he wouldn't like it. Instead, he began the out-of-phase launch sequence. Soon the lander was blasting off, scarring the xenolith and vaporizing methane excrudescences. The planet's surface fell dizzyingly away, and the rock with its hole was soon lost in a landscape that flattened and then curved back as the lander reached orbit. Vulpes knew that once he logged back in alone, the ship's systems would automatically plot a course back to Earth. Once aboard, and after a few vague housekeeping tasks were completed, the only thing to do would be to submit to suspension.

Given the terrible words in the encyclopedia entry, which Sevin had strove to alter in vain, Vulpes felt a hollow pang of satisfaction as he filed the ansible report, beaming back to Earth the strange details of their ordeal—and his survival. He couldn't place himself in suspension right away, however—the thought of even its sublime oblivion made him shudder—and for days he padded along throughout the compartments while OGLE-350c receded into the interstellar distances. One thought solaced him: when he was a boy, his grandfather said that the Internet of old was fickle and unstable, a fount of myths and lies; Wikipedia especially never could be trusted.

I AFTER THE CLOUDY DOUBLY BEAUTIFULLY

Before the turn of the millennium when the Web was new, I worked in the bowels of Harvard's Widener Library. There was as yet no Twitter, no Facebook, no YouTube; blogs and wikis were the glamorous spells of a whispering cognoscenti. But a web there was—enough of one to encourage the library to send many books off to storage in dark, refrigerated warehouses, never to be read again. This was my work in the Widener deeps. I was one of Bradbury's firemen, almost—though instead of heat and flame, we used the cool buzz of networked catalogs to put the books out of reach.

Among the duties with which I had been charged was clearing out the "X-cage." I wish I had made up this name; I wish I had made it up and then discarded it in embarrassment—alas, the X-cage was real. It was the repository of books, sheaves of paper, and artifacts in odd sizes and formats, of paper too fragile or content too salacious for the open stacks. Some of these I sent away to be stored elsewhere, while others I tried to place in more suitable libraries or museums. And some, frankly, I didn't know what to do with. My fascination with one such item has lingered through the years. Although it never was listed in the online system, I found it recorded in the card catalog while it still could be browsed in the library's attic. The card reads as follows:

Benjamin, Walter. Übersetzung Maschine. 1946.
Gift of le bibliothèque Orléans, Fr.

The device was housed in a case the size and shape of a largish briefcase, which led me to wonder: could it in fact have been the valise Benjamin carried with him in his flight over the Pyrenees? But the catalogue card contained no further information, and it's useless now to speculate.

The device itself looked for all the world like an Underwood typewriter, at once sleek and erect. In place of the roller carriage, however, rose a stately glass dome, like that on a ticker tape machine (when inverted, the dome stores cunningly in the cavity of the machine). Peering inside the glass dome, one glimpsed a reservoir of steel ball bearings each of which proved, upon closer inspection, to carry a letter in raised, reverse relief. The bearings appeared to travel through finely-milled grooves in a sleek steel cartridge, which slid out of the base of the machine; a bit of machine oil made the whole operation very smooth. There was one of these machined cartridges for each of the languages represented: German, English, French, Spanish, and Portuguese.

I oiled the parts, fitted to the assembly the carriage marked *Deutsch*, and began gingerly to type. W—I found that—A—each key went down with a ratchety resistance—L—and would not rebound until—D—the crank on the side of the machine was pulled—at which point the depressed keys all rose like clockwork and the works of the device flung the bearings about like popcorn in the dome, making an unbelievable racket. Finally the bearings settled, several of them having landed in a narrow steel track in the back of the machine. At the press of the RETURN key (on which the word *Zurückgehen* was marked in a thick *fraktur* type) the balls were rolled against a narrow paper tape; the tape advanced, the balls rolled down the track to rejoin their fellows, and the machine stood ready for another word. And I found that the paper tape as it clicked its way out of the machine carried the word WOODLAND in plain type.

I wondered, of course, about the machine's authenticity. I find only circumstantial evidence for it in Benjamin's own writings. In "The Work of Art in the Age of Mechanical Reproduction," Benjamin famously recognizes the loss of "aura" that attends the mechanical reproduction of art. He hopes, however, that freedom of access to the means of art's production might ultimately compensate us for this loss. If, furthermore, we can say that the differences among the languages, whatever beauty they may have, are ultimately to be counted among the tools of oppression and division— of Fascism in Benjamin's own time—then putting the means of effecting their negation into the hands of the masses surely would have appealed to Benjamin.

It was 1998 when I stumbled upon the *Übersetzungmaschine*; the internet bubble was still expanding, and new sites and features expanded the Web's imperium from week to week. The latest "tool" to arrive on the scene was a network-based machine translation service called Babelfish (on the Alta Vista search site, now long defunct). In a *Feed* magazine review of Babelfish, technoculture critic Julian Dibbell explored the tantalizing and esoteric possibilities of machine translation, noting the uncanny fact that in Babelfish translations "there (was) no flash of mystery that (couldn't) be traced to a mechanical arithmetic of words made into numbers." Dibbell recognized that Babelfish at its heart was a mystical enterprise, seeking to smooth out the postlapserian confusion of the tongues: "We can certainly say that where, throughout its history, translation has veered between the two extremes of license and literalism, seeking at its best a middling compromise, Babelfish manages the unprecedented feat of attaining both ends simultaneously."

Reading this, Benjamin's Translation Machine suddenly seemed plausible—and not merely plausible; it had been the beginning of a mighty enterprise. After all, the hope for a machine that kabbalistically reproduces language (and with it, the universe) has deep roots, stretching back through Erasmus Darwin's speech machine, through Jonathan Swift's "Discourse Concerning the Mechanickal Operation of the Spirit," to the *Mysterium Magnum* of the mystic Jacob Boehme. Now I was excited to try the translation machine on a real text, and returned to the X-cage to search for something appropriate. A nearby box proved to be jammed full of pamphlets and chapbooks from Alfred *Jarry's College de 'Pataphysique*; I yanked out the tiny, triangular booklet containing Jarry's chanson *"Tatane"*:

Chanson/pour faire/rougir/les negres/et/glorifier/le Pere Ubu

1. "Ne me chicane
Ce seul cadeau:
Jamais tatane
Dans le dodo!"

2. Lors reste en panne
Je ne sais ou
Un diaphane
En caoutchouc . . .

As I entered the above stanzas from the first page of the book-let, my enthusiasm flagged. The technicians of the early machine age were not exactly ergonomically aware, and the energy required to depress the keys took its toll. My carpal tunnels aflame, I pulled the lever one last time and tore out the tape, which read as follows:

Tatane Song to make redden the negres and glorifier the Ubu Father

1. "does not baffle me
This only gift:
Never trotter-case
In the dodo!"

2. At the time broken down remainder
I do not know
or diaphanous
Out of rubber . . .

The translation that results at first glance appeared as literally word-for-word as could be. But in these provisional gropings, the machine was reaching for the ineffable. It took the broken and inexpressive words in Jarry's poem and searched out mundane replacements—thereby alienating the text further from the target language than the avant-garde original. As "tatane" becomes "trotter-case," and "caoutchouc" shifts to "Out of rubber," we're brought into contact with the jumble of paradox that plays behind language's staid, everyday façade. I wasn't surprised—for to Benjamin, the word itself was the mere ground of the translation, granting entrée to the expansive mystery of the Word itself. As he writes in his "the Task of the Translator":

> A real translation is transparent; it does not cover the original, does not block its light, but allows the pure language, as though reinforced by its own medium, to shine upon the original all the more fully. This may be achieved, above all, by a literal rendering of the syntax which proves words rather than sentences to be the primary element of the translator. For if the sentence is the wall before the language of the original, literalness is the arcade.

It's this arcade of literalness through which the user of Benjamin's translation device ambles, a *flâneur* gratefully lost in the significatory flux that exists among the languages—which is, in fact, according to Benjamin, the primordial medium that exists prior to language, prior to the cataclysm of Babel:

> In this pure language—which no longer means or expresses anything but is, as expressionless and creative Word, that which is meant in all languages—all information, all sense, and all intention finally encounter a stratum in which they are destined to be extinguished.

Determined to use Benjamin's machine as it had been intended—by extinguishing information, sense, and intention in a pure language—it occurred to me that the operation of Benjamin's machine could take place any number of times over the same text, exchanging the language cartridges again and again, retranslating cyclically, algorithmically. This might have the effect of putting the languages themselves in dialogue, as it were, about the very nature of this pure language. To test this, I wanted a text that was both richer and more lexically and syntactically coherent than "*Tatane*"; my eyes seized upon an early, hand-bound Viennese edition of Goethe's 1789 *Schriften*, and I began laboriously to enter the first lines of the Dedication:

Der Morgen kam; es scheuchten seine Tritte
Den leisen Schlaf, der mich gelind umfing,
Daß ich, erwacht, aus meiner stillen Hütte
Den Berg hinauf mit frischer Seele ging;
Ich freute mich bei einem jeden Schritte
Der neuen Blume die voll Tropfen hing;
Der junge Tag erhob sich mit Entzücken,
Und alles war erquickt mich zu erquicken . . .

which the 1983 *Selected Poems*, edited by Christopher Middleton, has as follows:

The morning came, away its footfall sent
The gentle sleep that floated lightly o'er me,
So wide awake out of my hut I went
And gaily up the mountain slope before me.

At every stride I took, the flowers tender,
Brimming with dew, a pleasure were to see;
The young day sprang to life in all its splendour,
And everything seemed glad to gladden me . . .

I continued to feed in the German text, on to the sixty-fourth line. Then I tore out the printed tape, switched cartridges from English to German, and began to type again. My reiterative translation took a week to produce, and I only managed six cycles, German to English and back again, before I became too exhausted to continue. Here's my last English translation:

The morning came; scheuchten its job paragraph, to which the peace sleep wakes up, which I easily, which I clasped, my calm hut, which the mountain with fresh soul went over; I was fallen with each job paragraph of the new flower, which drops hung completely; The new day rose with Entzuecken, and everything was renews me, in order to renew. And during I rose, from the river of the meadows drew nebula eight out into the strip. It accessories and to the river modified and grew winged me too around over precedes: 'I not are not to enjoy the beautiful opinion somehow longer, the area covered for me a cloudy Flor; Soon I saw from the clouds, how Bekehrte surrounded and with me, if they dawn at one time seemed the sun into the fog for reached through to the left a clarity longs. Here it sant calmly for diverson; Here ' it theilt, which rises around forest and Hoehn. Receive how hopes' I it the first greeting! She hopes 'I after the cloudy doubly beautifully. Luft'gekampf for a long time, do not surround a gloss, which I was executed and I dazzled. Soon I for breaking the eyes open innrerantrieb the inside again courageously, i-konnt, for which ' it is formed only with fast opinion Trauen, because everything also seemed for burning and gluehn. There goettlich, which forwards central eyes to a swum Mrs, no beautiful figures I in my life overvoltage, you, regard which I saw and remained, to the Swimming of the Remains with the carried clouds. Don't you know me? she spoke with an opening, this all dear ' and Loy

The essential purity of this translation speaks for itself, I think. While the 1983 translation enfolds Goethe's Romantic German in a nostalgic English—triangulating among inversions and archaisms and the free line of modern prosody—the machine produces a glossolalic howl, a gift of the tongue in a voice at once bacchic and prophetic. Where the 1983 version has "gaily up the mountain slope before me,"—which, despite its faithfulness to the "information" of the original, can't help being too tritely bucolic—the machine, with concision bordering on impaction, gives us "which the mountain with fresh soul went over." German words glow here like gems on the ground of a deutschified English. And the English itself often seems pulled from these words like the entrails from a fowl: the sentence "Luft'gekampf for a long time, do not surround a gloss, which I was executed and dazzled" is the ideal example of this phenomenon, and manages to constitute a manifesto of translation in the process. And Goethe's "Tritte" or footsteps, and "Schritte" or steps—a delicate modulation, which the 1983 version strives to emulate—the machine ruthlessly pares down to an essential unity in the startling phrase "job paragraph." By resorting to pure language, we can see that Goethe is writing the world with his very strides.

My appetite was whetted. It now occurred to me that if I ran a text through each cartridge in succession, then all the languages could engage in the conversation at once. Exhausted by the Goethe, I chose a shorter text: Milton's 1633 verse translation of Psalm I:

Bless'd is the man who hath not walk'd astray
In counsel of the wicked, and ith' way
Of sinners hath not stood, and in the seat
Of scorners hath not sate. But in the great
Jehovah's Law is ever his delight,
And in his Law he studies day and night.
He shall be as a tree which planted grows
By watry streams, and in his season knows
To yield his fruit, and his leaf shall not fall,
And what he takes in hand shall prosper all.
Not so the wicked, but as chaff which fann'd
The wind drives, so the wicked shall not stand
In jugdment, or abide their tryal then,
Nor sinners in th'assembly of just men.
For the Lord knows th' upright way of the just,
And the way of bad men to ruine must.

Running through all the cartridges in succession, from English to French to German to Portugese to Spanish and back home to English, I produced the following translation:

Bless ' d é human beings, em avocats that moinhos you conseils misdirected ' athd não vêem or bad and do ith ' do innershath não caught and not scornershath do assento, em ordem for não to satisfer itself. But em great Jehovahs to law é never seu to prazer, and em sua law examines or day and prejudica-o. Não will return or seu, of like uma árvore, of which plantem or increase hair atrywuerfe, and em seu branco gives estaÁão, em winch of sua fruit and suas you are gives page, and or that face exame nonregulamento, to prosper all. Bad, but like Flitter that fann ' d or vento gives attempt, assim, for manter- bad like nenhuns not jugdment não também ou nele do remains tryal então, sinners imóveis joint do th internal ' two homens right. For or cavalheiro vê knows stops to direita or th of hardly, and to maneira of homens maus na ruína deve.

In this translation the languages weave among each other like dancers around a maypole, exchanging tenses and inflections and making light of homophony. The words themselves fall like angels through the void, swerving in Lucretian, meaning-making trajectories. The "counsels of the wicked" become so many "conseils misdirected," and then the language pulls back like a curtain to reveal that the Lord Himself is a prancing "cavalheiro." As Benjamin once wrote, commenting on Genesis 1:27:

> God created man from the word, and he did not name him. He did not wish to subject him to language, but in man God set language, which had served him as a medium of creation, free.

But here my investigation broke off. I had hopes to continue the work, putting to the task all the power of the computer technology that, in Benjamin's time, had not yet disclosed itself. The algorithmic potential of the computer to reiterate these translations thousands, even millions of times, may bring us to the very brink of the territory Benjamin describes:

> Translation does not find itself in the center of the language forest but on the outside facing the wooded ridge; it calls into it without entering, aiming at that single spot where the echo is able to give, in its own language, the reverberation of the work in the alien one.

Translation is always an amalgam of hope and nostalgia, combining the yearning for home with the urge to press forward into new territories. William Brenner, writing about the *Philosophical Investigations*, wonders if Wittgenstein doesn't come to understand language as a kind of colonial outpost on the edge of a great wilderness. Perhaps there is a harmony here, in the language mysticism of Benjamin and Wittgenstein: the several human languages are so many outposts, and the wilderness is this inexpressible, pure language about which Benjamin writes.

If my thoughts on these issues are muddled, my enthusiasm was keen; alas, the *Übersetzungmaschine* was not to remain my plaything for long. Other duties took me from the X-Cage for a time; one day while running an errand, I noticed a familiar case on the library loading dock, stuck with a delivery label that indicated an address in Mountain View, CA. I wanted to spirit the package away—but the dock was busy, and the package was soon on its way.

In the intervening years, Babelfish wriggled deep into the Internet's ear canal, becoming a virtual engine on the Web and desktops that automatically translates digitally-encoded texts into the increasingly polyglot English of globalization. In his Feed article, Julian Dibbell had wondered if Babelfish wouldn't expand the horizons of literary creation. In this, I don't think he was far from an incipient truth—a tantalizing and unnerving prospect, like the "bitistics" of Stanislaw Lem's fictions—a machine-created literature of the conscious supercomputers, which seeks to complete the incompleteness of human literary works. "For this literature," Lem wrote, "which has taken nothing from us apart from language, humanity appears not to exist."

In fact, I don't fear the prospect; I like to imagine such a literature becoming the vehicle of an avant-garde language mysticism. In Benjamin's machine—in its reiterative translation, multiplied millions of times in computers—I glimpsed a kind of auto-mystical reading practice erotic in its fixation, masturbatory in its repetitiousness. It seemed something from the dreams of Georges Bataille—who, as keeper of the Library at Orléans, might well have been the librarian who preserved Benjamin's machine for us during the darkest years of the war. And couldn't the primordial flux of pure language, modulated and spun for us by our ever-faster computers, someday become the very medium of our own literature? Wherein works will reside simultaneously in all their possible translations, to be plucked spinning from the void, viewed, and thereby determined, like so many quantum particles.

PASSAGES

CHILDREN OF THE VOLCANO

It is said that there is no mention of volcanoes anywhere in the Icelandic sagas; when Eyjafjallajökull erupted in 2010, stranding travelers in airports throughout Europe, their absence seemed a pregnant one.

As the Landnámabok tells it, in 1010 AD the sorcerers Hilmir and Hrafn moved in next to each other below the glacier on good flat land where they raised their sheep and chased the trolls from underneath their neighbors' rocks. But one day there was smoke on the mountain and fire in the ice, and a flood came storming down from the glacier. Hrafn stood behind his walls of stone and threw spells to turn the waters away from his flocks towards Hilmir's land. Hilmir climbed to his roof and sang for all he was worth; but his spells were late and his runes weak, and the flood swept away his flocks, his rocks, his home. Hilmir took the whale's road to Norway and his story dropped from the sagas.

Not long after, Katla the witch built her hut with the help of her son Odd high on the slopes of the mountain. Odd was strong and simple and quick; when one of Hrafn's sons took a ewe from him, he swept off his hand with a scythe. Katla tried with all her spells to hide Odd, and although his sons' wits were sundered by Katla's craft, Hrafn's art was strong and he saw through the witch's rude magic. With a spell of his own—Odin's magic, rune-magic—he set the very stones of Katla's hut afire. But then burning gold flowing down the mountain loosed an angry tide of cold water to quench the were flames. Katla perished, whether of flame or flood none could tell. But Odd disappeared in the mist of ash, and his story dropped from the sagas.

A thousand years later, Tinna Guðnasdottir, Odd's great-granchild seven times over, sits in a boarding lounge in Schipol with her legs propped on her rolling suitcase and the fey glimmer of Spring's late twilight on her face. She was due to leave for New York three days ago. But instead she's still in Amsterdam, and she's staring into the eyes of Neils Ullman—Neils of Minot, North Dakota, whom she had never met until yesterday. He was planning to backpack across India. But Neils isn't so sure now—for in Tinna's black eyes he spies glimmers of molten gold and storms of glass. Tinna taught him to say the name—*Eyjafjallajökull*—the syllables strangely soft and sharp like spells made not of runes but flowing fire and flood. And now he wants to see the land that his great-grandfather seven times over left so long ago when he swore off spellmaking and woolgathering and came over the whale's road to Norway.

THE DARKLING PLAIN

The origin of these prairies has caused much speculation. We might as well dispute about the origin of the forests, upon the assumption that the natural covering of the earth was grass. Probably one-half of the earth's surface, in a state of nature, was prairies or barrens. Much of it, like our western prairies, was covered with a luxuriant coat of grass and herbage. The steppes of Tartary, the pampas of South America, the savannas of the southern, and the prairies of the western states, designate similar tracts of country. Mesopotamia, Syria, and Judea had their ancient prairies, on which the patriarchs fed their flocks. Where the tough sward of the prairie is once formed, timber will not take root. Destroy this by the plough, or by any other method, and it is soon converted into forest land. There are large tracts of country in the older settlements, thirty or forty years since the farmers mowed their hay, that are now covered with a forest of young timber of rapid growth.

Clouds stand in for landscape and hills are prodigies, monsters, dragons' teeth. A picket of young trees stood on the verge of a timber that festered in the crook where street met highway at the edge of town. The timber was watered by a creek that passed under the highway through a great concrete tunnel—more like hallway than tunnel in its square cross-section. Slip down a bank of grass tresses to enter the tunnel, the timber's uncanny entryway. Through the timbered fretwork beyond its cool wall spy a dun sheen of grass, a forgotten quilt of prairie stitched by orb spiders and the vagrant thrushes. Within the tunnel, a dimpled vitrine of water glazed the floor, strands of algae pointing the way, festooning the cracks and machine-made jointures of masonry. Smack-smack-smack through the tunnel towards the timber's green light, swishing foot-falls seeming first to hurry forward in echoes that stuttered ahead through time, only to reverse course and hang back timidly in the midst. Finally a breathing-out, green glow mellowing to white of sky through the besom of the trees.

Summer Bible camp at a white church in a timber primordially green, a tangled garden sprung up in a corn-barren cleft. Its flower-jeweled particularity was wasted on most of the mouth-breathing surlies in summer exile. The kinds of timber most abundant are oaks of various species, black and white walnut, ash of several kinds, elm, sugar maple, honey locust, blackberry, linden, hickory, cotton wood, pecaun, mulberry, buckeye, sycamore, wild cherry, box elder, sassafras, and persimmon. It would have been miserable but for a girl a year older made of blond and china who picked a bucket of blackberries. They seemed to bud forth and ripen at her touch. The trees would have gone to war for her. The fire annually sweeps over the prairies, destroying the grass and herbage, and blackening the surface, and leaving a deposit to enrich the soil. And there aren't enough blackberries in the world.

The town was an unaccountable *ultima thule* deep-folded amid fields of soybean and corn. For five hundred miles in any direction the land had been planed by continental blades of ice, which carved the great lakes and left mile-wide rivers rolling stones and icebergs down their tumblings. But some obscurer forces had kneaded the hilly defile where a surveyor had come to spread out gridded lots like a quilt draped over picnic goods. In a standard-issue town somewhere on the high prairie, some flattened grid of black streets bubbling in the August sun, the anomaly of the hills would never have presented itself; in some high country, the rhythm of ridge and hollow would have seemed merely de rigueur. But here the impertinent hills, measured out by history, looked out on a river and trees and the dull horizon.

The suck and trickle of the paddle playing counterpoint with the hum of the mercury vapor lamp at the corner of the parking lot overhanging the bend in the river at the edge of town. Look back; the tumble-milled cobbles of foreign granite died like stars in the evening murk while the canoe's aft end swung out into the middle of the river trailing ragged black parentheses across the water's dimpled top. Behind the graying shore, shadows massed: propane tank, tree of heaven, and the night's enveloping leaves, parted here and there by the flickering prick of streetlights in town. Swiveling, sliding into place on the vinyl seat, watch the bow as it bobs plumb with the current, aiming into the angle where dark trees tumbled down to the vanishing point and made a crotch of the star-furred sky. There should be hoots and slitherings in the brush. Instead, the only sounds are the lamp-hiss hung high on its pole and the plumbing of the river running through channels in the bottom of the canoe.

He slung along, wrist-twisting the paddle with each stroke to keep the boat moving in a straight line—tick tock tick back and forth across its course—and watched snags drift by in the peripheral gloom. The light was lowering, the tree-shadows closing in and down. Above, their leaf-crowns stood away to reveal gobbets of starlight amidst obscure constellations. Strange, he noted, the way the riverbanks drowned in darkness seemed to disappear, how the treetops, falsely solid in the night, seemed to become the banks of a deeper river along the bottom of which he slid and shuffled in his carapace-canoe.

There was the town, and then *the town*, mirrored in their habits. In the town, raiment of cottonwood down and willow, the oaks spilling golden seed on the barren roads of Spring amid the relentless sun. While in *the town*, angled shadow lit the homes in black, blackshine measures the stillborn road. We don't see *the town* from here; it angles off obscurely, a ricochet of time's obscure trajectory and the habit of the world. Could it be said to settle the reservoir, to haunt the waters beyond the lake fuzzed floor? Although to call it a "haunting" is to clothe it in a costume not its own, the habit of an accidental cosmos jealous of hints and vectors. He let the paddle go slack in his hands, felt the canoe nudged into a slow turn by the current. Looking over his shoulder he watched the last lights of town wink out among the obscure trees. Oh how it once poured through here, the water, rank and shriven, how it foamed brown and took down the trees in groves. A roar five miles wide though miles were never measured then; nor was the measure of the roar taken either, at least not by human ears. This after the scouring of the ice, amidst the agelong wandering of the north magnetic pole and the steady restless shrugging of the constellations. These ponderous rhymes through the slow-metered stilling of the planet's fires, the compass rose dialing to rest, the stilling churn and convection. All this making unmade, innocent of the appearances. Steppe rising upon steppe in a land undenominated into prairie, of wilderness, and road, steppe upon steppe upon steppe unto higher green countries of blown ash and glaciers where locusts fat with the teeming cud of unflowered plants, fall from the sky, entomb themselves in ice for undreamt of creatures to walk and puzzle over in doomed ages to come.

But little has been done to introduce cultivated grasses. The prairie grass looks coarse and unsavory, and yet our horses and cattle thrive well on it. It is already known to the reader that this grass disappears when the settlements extend round a prairie, and the cattle eat off the young growth in the spring. Consequently in a few years, the natural grass no longer exists.

AN APOCALYPSE

It was the end of the world, and no one took notice. They boy who rode in the back of the truck with a weapon between his knees carried a secret in his head, lodged in places he couldn't unlock except through the invisible lockwork of time and experience. The secret wasn't even the secret, but only the means of its discovery—an access of insight into a power that would remake the world. Its possibility was hardly seminal, much less instantiate, a spiral angel that slumbered in the cells. It slumbered while he sat in the back of the truck bouncing on his bones with the rest of the crew. He fingered the action on his weapon; he worked it in and out, the machined levers and pins sliding together and apart with easy imperfection, like the last few teeth in an old man's mouth. Such spirits had been formulated throughout history; while most had been snuffed out, some had flowered forth in blossoms of insight. *Why do you keep working the bolt like that?* a companion asked him. Such an inflorescence would have filled up the boy, who was soft and dreamhaunted despite his lean limbs and his haughty mouth; it would have put him before his brethren and led them through him to see themselves with something close enough to truth. *The sound makes a kind of color,* he said without glancing up to watch the foliage stream by sickeningly as the truck sped down the forest track. *I see green, and happy machines.* Which is all that would have served to save the world, in the end: the simplest insight truly born and placed before one and all to catch in its light the reflection of the world at its every point. In their millions, people would have laughed at the simplicity of the salvation he showed them to, which would prove in time to be their apotheosis as well: the way that the forces which they worshipped as gods were selfish and all-seeing and tormented by hunger, while the truth which shaped them was blind in its devotion to their perfection. He would have taught them; he would have taught *us*. Now it's given to us only to know this much, even if we're doomed now to remain ignorant of the means by which the deed would have been accomplished, how the insight would have turned aside the weapon-making and the disease-seeding and set our kind on its course toward the stars. *It makes a kind of color*, his companion said, snickering and turning to face the others who sat in the back of the truck, a fat man with a shotgun and a trembling, wall-eyed man with one hand. And the round was through him while its sound still rent the air, a large-calibre shell that tore through the wall of the truck, deflected and blossomed into an ugly cleaver, and bore into the boy, breaking his back and destroying his liver. It was at this point that the world ended, that its fate was sealed, that the course was set upon which its demise would be composed in heat and storms of broken glass. And no one noticed; no one could have known. His knees buckled and the weapon clattered and the head with its stillborn angel of transcendence and escape struck the bloodsmeared bed with a sound like the crack of a bell. Of course the end itself would take time; it would patiently measure itself out in dessication and ruin and finally, finally in silence. Just now, the truck sped up. Arriving at the camp in the forest, the others made the one-handed man drag the boy's body to a trench where he struggled to shovel it over with lime.

THE UNICORN

Allen Dwiggins lived by himself in a brick townhouse in an old, forgotten neighborhood. A graphic designer, he went to work each day in a building overlooking a network of sluices of quick-running river water which, having once excited the city's industry, now dashed picturesquely past streets and under bridges. On the weekends Allen went for long walks in a cemetery at the edge of his neighborhood—a vast and rambling necropolitan suburb with bending cypresses and weeping beeches and exotic specimens of spruce from the far east—a quiet, sylvan surround decorated with softly-carved crosses, prim statues of Grace, and mausoleums like gothic garden sheds.

Amidst this memorial splendor one Saturday morning, Allen met a unicorn. It was a sunny, bracing day in early Spring; he was sitting on a low rock wall listening to a flock of chickadees rustle in a nearby bush when the unicorn walked out from behind a great rock and clumsily folded itself into a knot at his feet.

The unicorn was spectacularly ugly. Swollen and thickly-jointed, it reminded Allen of a rhinoceros rather than the gracile equine of the old tapestries. The size of a middling hog, its hide was grayish-green, carbuncled, and hairless but for a few thin, coarse strands sprung from its spinal harrow and plastered here and there to its sides. In place of a mane it sported a bristle that was wiry, close-cropped, and thick enough of knap to scrub a ship's hull. Its tail was no silky brush but a wrist-like, twisted stump that ended abruptly in a shrubby tangle of hair. Its eyes, wracked and inflamed, were yellow and bulging and punctuated with a black iris. But the horn, the horn was the thing: no flute of ivory and spun gold but a blade of obsidian, glossy and black, which rose to a narrow, jagged point. Its hooves—which it must be admitted were properly cloven—were of the same adamantine cast.

The unicorn looked up, its whiskered eyelids twitching. Allen felt a chill of anxiety run down his legs; the chickadees had gone still, and the whole scene, the wall of puddingstone and the bruised grass and the vacuous graves, seemed to gather around the unicorn's pricked and empty eye, pressing in and locking together in a glimmering tunnel of vertigo. Allen could put no name to the sensation—this vague desire absent the pressure of longing, this quietude at once active and rooted, settled in time and place. The unicorn blinked, and its mouth wrenched itself into a blistering grin.

After a time the unicorn broke their mutual gaze, rose stiffly, and ambled about. It made no sound other than a high nasal rooting, which it emitted while snuffling windblown leaves gathered into the margins of the hedges. In subsequent visits, Allen found that the beast never tired of these browsings, although it never seemed to glean anything edible in the process.

It had a disconcerting habit of stopping every now and again to fix its gaze on a headstone. At first Allen wondered: could the creature be reading? Could it be sussing out the vital facts of the entombed, pondering their mortal traces? It was just as happy examining the backs of the stones as it was the graven fronts, however, and after a few such episodes, Allen concluded it was not genealogy but geology that captured the beast's interest. And while it never tried to communicate, its uncanny eyes were always full of something Allen that supposed looked like love. Whenever Allen would resume his walk through the cemetery the unicorn would follow for awhile, mincing along on its quick splayed legs like a pug-dog in high-heeled shoes. But it would never travel far from the low rock wall with the bird-bustling hedge. Allen would climb a low rise or turn a corner, and the knotty, esoteric creature would be gone.

It took no time at all for Allen to become attached to the unicorn and their uncanny, silent ramblings. One Spring evening he stayed in the cemetery past closing. The unicorn's eyes glowed faintly, reflecting and concentrating the evening's crepuscular glow. It was a moonless night, and only a few stars appeared to prick the darkening orange tarp of the sky.

"Does it bother you that the sky is so empty?" Allen asked aloud, craning his neck. The unicorn vented a weak, baritone croak and settled into its customary crouch. "It's always disappointed me. That's not how it looks in the textbooks, on public television, in science museums. There it's all toroid clouds of stars blown apart, lacy rings a thousand light years across, galaxies spinning and glowing in a thousand colors. But it never really looks like that, does it, the sky? Instead it's just points of light, unchanging, very faint. The scientists use special lenses and software and equipment to make those pictures. But wherever you go in the universe, you look with your own eyes and all you'll see are those faint points of light, always unbearably far away."

He looked down at the unicorn, its eyes nebulizing, titrating the light. "Animals are like that, too," Allen continued. "They're always faint and faraway. It's not just that nature is mostly empty space. It's that everything is repelling everything else."

The unicorn settled it head stiffly, stacking its wide snout atop its forehocks and shutting its pixellated eyes. A sheen of starlight swirled in its mirrored horn.

If the unicorn had any idea of Allen's considered notions, it never disclosed them. The two continued their idle tours, however, and inevitably, others noticed the unlikely pair. Dogwalkers would approach in amity only to find themselves tugging at the leashes of their dogs, who lay themselves at the unicorn's scalpeled feet in mute, quivering submission. Most walkers changed course urgently, and Allen found himself ever more scrupulously avoiding funeral gatherings for fear of disconcerting the mourners. As weeks passed and the weather warmed, however, passersby traded revulsion for curiosity in increasing numbers. It was only a matter of time before a video of Allen and his fey companion went viral.

And so it came one bright morning that Allen found himself on the rock wall, the unicorn staring off into space at his side, while a mob of reporters crowded in on them baying and clamoring for answers. They asked him what the unicorn did and what its habits were; they asked when it came to him, and whether it observed any schedule or phases or rituals; they asked how it survived, whether it grazed the grasses or browsed the bushes or consumed meaner, perhaps unspeakable meals; finally, they asked Allen why. Why did the unicorn choose him?

Allen had pondered this question many times but had never yet felt bold enough to answer. His gaze drifted as he considered, and his eyes came to rest on a reporter's tablet computer lying in the long grass playing an astronomical screen saver. It was high summer, and the reflection of clouds in the blue sky played across the sheen as planets and galaxies toiled in the tablet's glossy void.

Allen thought of nature and the starry sky and everything he had said to the placid unicorn a few nights before. But all he managed was, "I don't know." And then, feeling stupid about it before the words ever left his mouth, "It's a gift."

It's not because you're a virgin, is it? came a cry from the back of the group, prompting vague chortles.

The reporters began to rustle and hum, absorbed in their own colloquy; Allen sat listening, hands laced together in his lap. The unicorn browsed at their feet, sniffing here and there; when it came to the tablet computer it looked down, curious, and placed one cloven hoof in the middle of the screen, which broke with a sharp snap and a little puff of smoke. Everyone fell silent as the reporter picked up her tablet and turned it over in her hands, examining it from all angles. The gadget still functioned, but its galaxies and star clusters spun now in splintery shards. Text and image alike now appeared in puzzles, like leaves of origami folded and rudely flattened.

The unicorn wandered away, as was its wont; and soon the journalists too disappeared, hying off to their own secret haunts. Allen watched as the unicorn fell to the ground and commenced snuffling the stump of its tail. "Oh that was very nicely done," he said to the self-absorbed mythical beast.

Allen wrote the reporter offering to pay for her broken tablet, but she told him not to bother. A few weeks later he received another email: the gadget was still working, even though she hadn't charged it in all that time. In a shattering of capacitive glass, the unicorn's touch had imparted to the gadget some source of undying energy.

Soon the story was all over the news. Pilgrims made their way to the cemetery, bringing their gadgets in hopes of receiving the unicorn's blessing of unending power. Things got unmanageable for awhile; Allen and the unicorn appeared on talk shows (always shot on location at the cemetery, as the unicorn would never travel), and there was a harrowing episode involving a Russian mobster who wanted to harvest the unicorn's glassy, fragile horn. Those episodes came and went, the kind of thing you read about in the news. And in about a year and half, scientists had reverse-engineered the unicorn's secret, making gadgets with endlessly renewable power sources accessible to anyone with a credit card. The world changed, not as much as anyone had hoped.

After that, interest in Allen and his ugly little unicorn dwindled. Once explained, commodified, and made scalable, the unicorn's secret had lost its glamor. But for occasional gawkers, pilgrims stopped coming to the cemetery. Allen went back to designing logos and arranging type on screens whose energies now never flagged; in renovated solitude he repaired to the habit of his walks, perambulating the cemetery twice a week save when illness or errands prevented it. Regularly he sat on the rock wall with the ugly little unicorn at his side watching the seasons come and go.

And so it continued as Allen grew old and infirm; and one day he couldn't walk anymore; and one day he died. And still the unicorn watched by the rock wall: the seasons turned, blending into harshness year by year; headstones fell over and crumbled into dust; trees, shattering amidst the graves in ones and twos, were replaced by spiny vegetation with ground-hugging habits in ever more sere shades of green. Those plants withered, too, and were not replaced. Snow fell, ice rose and retreated; snow fell and the ice rose again and sublimed. And still the unicorn watched; it watched as clouds of oxygen bubbled and flared green on the edges of galaxies; watched a billion suns wheel and fall into immense black holes; watched star clusters collide and die and fade into glowing storms of gas and the unicorn could see all these things, for the unicorn it all seemed unbearably close at hand.

THE WORLD & THE TREE

Before my journey I hesitated to commit to writing my views concerning the Tree, which heretofore was the world, for they were heterodox in the extreme, and I was not eager to lose the esteem of good friends. Nonetheless as this age draws to a close and things cease to be as they always have seemed, I feel it necessary to put down in some form my objections to conventional wisdom concerning the Tree before complete ruin is upon us and all is truly lost. For I have reason to believe that Tree is *not* the world; that there was a time before the Tree, and yet there was a world; that there was a time when the Tree was merely *in* the world—a tree among trees, bordering great spaces in which *no tree at all was to be found.*

With these observations fresh before the mind, I acknowledge that the Tree's divine bounty cannot be discounted: its fine twigs furnish not merely kindling, but also the most remarkable cloth when shredded and spun; its garden limbs, frassed and shaggy with a hundred varieties of lichen, mosses, and mushrooms, where dead leaves and twigs and spent bark drift down and catch, turning to soil that sustains gardens of chokes and worts fed by fat worms; its broad branches leading on for league upon league through the canopy which, when cleaned and planed to living blond wood, make routes wide enough for wagons to drive two abreast; its great crooks and cavities where rainwater collects in placid pools or gushes in cataracts through the hollowed-out pillars of the trunks. But for the hissing stones which, fallen from the sky, are skeined in boughs to make our altars of memory, and the air and water (which are also of the sky), there is no material which is not wood, which is aught but the Tree transmuted.

How long our ancestors subsisted without shelter in the Tree, beyond that which the largest limbs could afford, cannot be known. But at some point in the primordial past, the miracle of the cutting was discovered—the subtle patterns of scoring, biting down through bark into the living cambium, out of which emerge the traceries and buttresses from which our storage huts houses, and great halls are grown. By these gentle woundings or ancestors discovered that the Tree would yield new swift-growing limbs, strong, ropelike vines, or a flourishing bouquet of fresh green twigs, depending on the subtle art with which the depth and density of the scoring was accomplished. Nestled mid-canopy, our settlements affect a symbiosis with the Tree that is necessary to the survival of the human species. Our very homes are carved and grown from the living tissue of the Tree; its rainwater catchments and lightly sweet sap hydrate and refresh us; its fruits and tender young shoots, together with a flourishing flora that festoons bark and limb, nourish our bodies. All the world's creatures—the flying dogs that caper and carom amidst the middle boughs, the fish teeming limb-crook pools, the butterflies that visit the hearkening blooms, even the all-but-immobile pythons wound around trunks in the sepulchral deeps, where they await the falling dead—all depend upon the Tree's bounty.

Only the great soaring birds, it seemed, subsisted beyond the beneficence of the Tree. We have no name for the birds, which have never been discovered roosting or alight; they only pass high overhead, rolling down the endless limbs of the clouds. It beggars belief to think that they never settle, that they only orbit forever in passage like planets amidst the far-off leaves of the stars. To watch the aloof grandeur of their migration—when at the equinoxes the great, black birds balloon from East to West in vast battalions—is to know an uncanny and alienating power. Few now climb to the Tree's very top to see their passage, however. I have made the journey—I have climbed beyond the shaped and tended boughs to where limbs grow upward into wild air, where the sunlight no longer filters through the leaves' living green but dissolves in the very atmosphere its golden heat. I have climbed the tallest branch, crooked and aged, and have looked out across the Tree's undulating canopy spreading out beneath the sky to see the masses of foliage mounding like clouds beneath the sun; I have watched the wind ripple the Tree in rolling gestures I cannot name, which measure off the leagues in shadows while the birds pass beyond reckoning.

The comprehensive and ubiquitous nature of the Tree seems to defy all attempts to draw limits around its extent or influence. With all the Tree offers and does—all the promises it long has kept—even to hint at skepticism or questions its infinitude provokes nervous energies of the highest order. Nonetheless my ideas concerning the Tree are founded upon not mere reflection, but empirical evidence.

And the birds offered my theories a sort of infernal hope. Wherever their passage led, the Tree was no part of it. To see that further world—to journey with the birds, to follow the winds through the boughs of the very clouds—this became my obsession.

Many years the kites have flown, gathering fire from the clouds to light our nights and brighten the Tree's encircling limbs. Their tethers rise, dipping and stretching as the sails drink the great currents of wind on high. And when lightning rends the black clouds and lights their very skeletons from within, the tethers crackle and glow. To make a journey by limb and branch as the seasons turned and the Tree went bare and the limbs went slippery with ice seemed beyond endurance; however, whenever I spied the kites making motes of themselves on high, I thought I glimpsed a way. And so I set to building a great kite—sharp and black, soft as the lichen-down from which it was woven, like one of the great birds themselves. And some ten lengths of a man from the kite, I wove myself into the tether line. From the heights to which the kite could pull me, I hoped, I could see farther than anyone had before.

It pulled me into the sky with astonishing force; quickly the canopy dropped away and the ripples of foliage flattened beneath me. Soon the Tree lay far below, an undulating skein of limb and leaf, its topmost mounds flattening into the whole, the tether snapping and singing in the wind, dropping away beneath me in an immense catenary curve to the trees far below. I had never been so distant from the boughs and leaves, and the estrangement combined with the height to carve out a hollow in my stomach. But as the tether stretched and tightened, it tore at the harness I had made to connect me to the kite; I heard the fibers of lichen as they creaked and began to break. In desperate hope that the kite would spiral softly downwards and return me to the Tree with little injury, I yanked out the small grafting knife from my belt and cut the tether.

I did not fall, but was vaulted upward viciously, borne aloft like a leaf amidst a rushing of air. Peeking in and out of the torn clouds faraway, the black kite spun, speaking in stutters to me through the wind-strummed rope. I was ripped up and up through a quilt of colder air before the kite and I settled into an uncanny train, the black sail measuring its distance in the plunging tether line, cold bands of rain slashing me like boughs across the face and body. And soon the clouds closed in and became a fog; drinking each breath from the ragged wind, I soon lost consciousness as time passed out of mind.

I awoke dangling, swinging almost imperceptibly in the in cold, wet air. Around me all was utterly black; I wondered if I had somehow crashed through the Tree in the night and now hung from the lowermost boughs in the deeps. My arms flamed numbly from the harness straps biting deep into my shoulder, and at first I could barely make them move. Shaking them back to life, I took hold of the tether line in both hands, and struggled to haul myself upwards. My palms burned from the coarse fiber of the rope when at last I thrust upward and struck my arm on what seemed to be a wrist-thick bough—only it was strangely cool, slippery, and resoundingly hollow, a thing made not grown. Grateful for the support, I swung a leg over the strange limb and hauled myself over. My leg slid onto a kind of ledge from which the thing jutted, and I cautiously backed myself onto what proved to be a broad, flat surface, gritty and broken, receding into darkness.

I lay there awhile gathering strength while the sun's thin light leaked over the horizon. Slowly the scene resolved around me: planed edges and sharp angles, solid surfaces polished to a watery sheen. As morning broke, an unanticipated spectacle lay spread beneath me: a canopy of limbshorn towering trunks of vast girth, seemingly fabricated from frozen water and piled into a vast pattern, dull and dazzling, planar like children's blocks, but enormous, stretching into misty distances. The scene was hemmed in on one horizon by a sight I had only glimpsed in dreams: the end of the Tree. A faraway thatch of boughs rested cloudlike atop a wall of buttressed trunks, which stretched upward to impossible heights from what even the shadows could not conceal was a massy surface, composed either of a fretwork of branches so deeply intertwined as to have been knit into a vast oneness, or a single limb of colossal, world-bearing size. Or so it appeared to my Treeborn eyes; I know it now to be the *omphalos mundi*, the limbless land, itself fallen from the sky —or perhaps falling now, and ever falling—that is the basis and origin of the Tree.

Before me lay a broken range of deadfall and ruptured blocks and prisms; whole trunks lay defeated amidst the ruins of some shattered, inscrutable industry. And between me and the Tree stretched this vast shardscape of fabricated towers, both built and broken, reflecting the morning in bright cards and patches of great size hanging in the very air. No wood, living or dead, lay close to hand; between where I stood and the uncanny, belief-beggaring edge of the Tree I could see neither wild bough nor worked living lumber, but only the piled-up mirrors and blocks and shields, shining and cool, but not cold enough to be frozen. And in all that vastness nothing stirred.

It was atop one of these built, frozen towers that I now stood, having caught by mere fortune on a kind of mast that stood out from the corners of its topmost edge. I found my way within—a door that shrieked on its hinges gave upon a dark shaft and stairs that led to the bottom, where horrid maze of rot-smelling hard walls led me out through more doors of shattered ice. Ruin lay everywhere:

shattered uncanny machines, surfaces like fire-hardened wood only cracked and riddled with holes; great gaping cavities overhung with brambles of strange, cutting branches of rough orange and the taste of blood. And everywhere in heaps or hanging in shards and blades, more of the frozen, strangely cool materials out of which the great towers were built.

I made my way through this shattered maze to the base of the Tree—though I could see clearly now that it was not one Tree but many, each vast in size but not so vast as the tumbled towers. There I gazed into the uncanny shadows that clung to the trunks and saw into the truth of the world and was shaken to the marrow. Somewhere high above, the sun was setting amidst the plaited scaffolding of the Tree. I gazed up into its dusky heights, my homeland, knowing now that it was after all not all my people had ever known. Someone had not grown but made the ruined towers, and then abandoned them for the Tree. Whether it had been opportunity or calamity was not given to me to know. Perhaps somewhere back in the figured labyrinth there were carvings or records to tell me.

When darkness fell, I made a fire, and slept in the hollow beneath a shattered trunk of the Tree. The night was filled with a sound of storm, like wind roaring in the finest branches, freshening and receding in a rhythmic, breath-like cycle.

In the morning the sun shone up the long, tortured defile where the piled towers and the Tree both came together. There was a brightness there, glimmering and vast, and I walked down to it. It took a long time, although the way was dizzyingly straight and plain; I was faint with hunger and footsore from long walking on flat surfaces. As I wandered down the broadening way, the sheen composes itself into a prodigious sight: a vast amount of water toiling and heaving in a body. Even the smell of the water was vast and rank; at its edge it foamed, angry and bright and heaving like some wounded beast, while up and down the lengths of its vastness trunks of the tree and shattered towers fell crashing and disappearing in its depths. And everywhere I looked, the black birds were crashing into the bright water, wheeling and dropping and diving, and when they rose to the surface their beaks flashed with fish gathered from below.

Now I live alone in the vast ruined habitation, and watch as day by day the Tree's trunks fall, widening the lumberyard of the world.

MATTHEW BATTLES writes about culture, science, and technology for the *Atlantic Monthly*, the *Boston Globe*, the *London Review of Books* and a host of other publications, and is a founder of HiLobrow, an online magazine of critical culture named one of the best blogs of 2010 by *Time Magazine*. His first book, *Library: an Unquiet History*, was translated into six languages. He lives in Boston, where he is a program fellow at Harvard's Berman Center for Internet and Society.

About the book and the process of publishing it

This is a Red Lemonade book, available in all reasonably possible formats—limited artisanal editions, in a trade paperback edition, and in all current digital editions, as well as online at the Red Lemonade publishing community at http://redlemona.de

A word about this community. Over my years in publishing, I learned that a publisher is the sum of all its constituent parts: yes and above all the writers, and yes, the staff, but also all the people who read our books, talk about our books, support our authors, and those who want to be one of our authors themselves.

So I started a company called Cursor, designed to make these constituent parts fit better together, into a proper community where, finally, we could be greater than the sum of the parts. The Red Lemonade publishing community is the first of these and there will be more to come—for the current roster of communities, see the Cursor website http://thinkcursor.com

For more on how to participate in the Red Lemonade publishing community, including the opportunity to share your thoughts about this book, read what others have to say about it, and share your own manuscripts with fellow writers, readers, and the Red Lemonade editors, go to the Red Lemonade website http://redlemona.de

Also, we want you to know that these sites aren't just for you to find out more about what we do, they're places where you can tell us what you do, what you want, and to tell us how we can help you. Only then can we really have a publishing community be greater than the sum of its parts.

As regards the participation of the Red Lemonade community in this book: Nora Nussbaum copyedited the manuscript; Susan Clements and the author proofread it.

Regards,

Richard Nash
Publisher